"Oh, but you'd look so handsome in a—"

Face reddening, Brooke pulled her lips between her teeth.

Heat infused Shaun's face, too, even as his chest swelled at the compliment. Before he realized he was going to ask, he blurted, "Any chance you'd save me from going stag?"

Her eyelids fluttered. "Wow. Wasn't expecting that."

"Just thought it would be more fun to attend with a friend, especially since we're both fairly new to town and probably won't…" He let the thought fade away.

"Yeah." The word came out on a sigh. She tucked her fingertips into her jeans pockets. "I'd love to attend the wedding with you. Thanks. Now I really must go shopping."

He thought she looked beautiful just as she was, paint-soaked jeans and all, and was about to tell her so before he abruptly came to his senses. Had he really been about to resort to shameless flirting? Because, seriously, this could go nowhere.

Nowhere.

Award-winning author **Myra Johnson** writes emotionally gripping stories about love, life and faith. She is a two-time finalist for the ACFW Carol Award and winner of the 2005 RWA Golden Heart® Award. Married since 1972, Myra and her husband have two married daughters and seven grandchildren. Although Myra is a native Texan, she and her husband now reside in North Carolina, sharing their home with two pampered rescue dogs.

Books by Myra Johnson

Love Inspired

Rancher for the Holidays
Her Hill Country Cowboy
Hill Country Reunion
The Rancher's Redemption
Their Christmas Prayer

Visit the Author Profile page at Harlequin.com.

Their Christmas Prayer

Myra Johnson

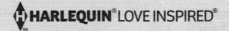

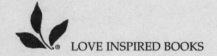

LOVE INSPIRED BOOKS

Recycling programs
for this product may
not exist in your area.

ISBN-13: 978-1-335-47946-4

Their Christmas Prayer

www.Harlequin.com

Printed in U.S.A.

For since the beginning of the world men have not heard, nor perceived by the ear, neither hath the eye seen, O God, beside thee, what he hath prepared for him that waiteth for him.

—Isaiah 64:4

For my family of pastors, pastors' wives and missionaries, all faithful servants of our awesome God: Peter and Johanna, Ben and Julena, Jim and Judy; and in memory of my late father-in-law, Reverend Lester Johnson.

Chapter One

After nearly fifteen years of overseas missionary service, Shaun O'Grady had picked up many handy skills. Ranching wasn't one of them. But since moving in a few weeks ago with Kent Ritter, the Texas cowboy soon to become his new brother-in-law, he was learning.

He'd just left the farm supply store with a bundle of push-in plastic fence posts and a roll of poly wire. On this chilly October morning, a steaming mug of coffee from Diana's Donuts sure seemed like a good idea. Being Saturday, the place was packed, and Shaun had to wait several minutes in line before he made it to the counter.

"Morning, Diana. One large black coffee, please." He tugged out his wallet. "Got any scones left?"

The ponytailed brunette peeked into the display case. "How does cranberry-walnut sound?"

"I'll take it." Shaun smiled his thanks as Diana handed him his order. Detouring to the condiment bar, he added a dollop of cream and grabbed some napkins as he scanned the shop for an empty table.

In the far corner, a couple of rancher types were getting up to leave. Shaun hurried to claim the table, but before he could set down his coffee and scone, a distracted-looking woman in business attire beat him to it.

"Oh!" Long honey-brown curls flipped across her shoulder as she looked up with a start. "Were you about to sit here?"

"No problem. I can…" Shaun took another look around. No more empty seats anywhere. Guess he could grab a to-go cup and take his coffee out to the pickup.

"You were in line ahead of me. You should take the table." The woman gathered up her coffee and Danish, only to be jostled by the customer in the chair behind her. She gasped as hot coffee splashed over the rim of her mug.

"Careful, there." Shaun set down his own mug and plate, then relieved the woman of hers. He thrust his fistful of napkins toward her. "Did you burn your hand?"

"I think it's okay. Startled me more than anything." She dabbed at a coffee spill on her slim plaid skirt. "So much for looking presentable for my meeting."

"Hardly shows," Shaun said with an encouraging smile. *They'll all be looking at your pretty face anyway.*

Whoa, did he actually just think that? True, she was incredibly attractive, not to mention the whole dressed-for-success vibe. Most of Diana's customers looked more like Shaun—faded jeans, dusty boots, weekend whiskers. Well, the guys, anyway.

He scraped a palm across his stubbly chin. "Hey, our coffee's getting cold and the crowd doesn't look like it'll be thinning out anytime soon. Would you be okay with sharing the table?"

Relief and gratitude replaced the disgruntled twist to her lips. "If you're sure you don't mind." She wadded up the napkins and offered her hand. "I'm Brooke Willoughby, your new chamber of commerce communications manager."

"Wow, that's a mouthful. Congratulations. I'm Shaun O'Grady, average guy in need of caffeine." No need to explain further. Besides, he didn't expect he'd ever have a reason to visit the Juniper Bluff Chamber of Commerce. After a quick handshake, they sat across from each other. "So, you're off to a business meeting?"

"I'm being officially introduced to the chamber's board of directors. And I'm a teensy bit edgy, as you can probably tell from my klutziness." She took a sip from her mug, then uttered a nervous laugh. "You might want to grab a few extra napkins in case I accidentally tip my coffee into your lap."

"I'll take my chances." Offering a grin, Shaun bit into his scone. "I'm wearing half the barnyard on these old jeans anyway, so who'd notice?"

Brooke's warm brown eyes sparkled with a knowing glint. "You must be a rancher, like just about everybody else in Juniper Bluff."

"Uh, that would be a no. I'm just staying with my sister's fiancé on his ranch until I figure out…" He tapped his heel. This wasn't a subject he particularly wanted to get into with a complete stranger. "I mean, I'm only in town temporarily."

"Oh, so you're not from Juniper Bluff. Neither am I. Until very recently, anyway. My mom died last year—"

"I'm so sorry."

"Thank you." The slightest tremor crept into Brooke's tone. "Anyway, my dad and I just moved here from Los Angeles. I had a great job at an advertising firm, but Dad really wanted to have the family close together again, so…" She gave a half-hearted shrug.

"I understand. Family's important." Family could also be meddlesome, as in insisting Juniper Bluff was the perfect place for Shaun to recover and regroup after burning out on the mission field. "You have relatives in town?"

"My brother. When he heard about the chamber of commerce position, he said it sounded perfect for me and insisted I apply. Next thing I knew, Dad and I were packed and hitting the road." Lifting a bite of pastry on her fork, she glanced toward the door. "Tripp was supposed to meet me here this morning, but he texted saying he got tied up at the clinic."

"He's a doctor?"

"A veterinarian."

Shaun nodded as pieces started falling together. "Tripp Willoughby—right. We met when he assisted Dr. Ingram with one of Kent's cows."

"Kent's your brother-in-law?"

"To-be. The wedding's Thanksgiving weekend." Shaun figured he could stick around at least that long. And maybe by then he'd have his head on straighter. He'd been praying desperately for direction about where his life was headed, but it seemed like God had gone silent.

"Last time I came to Juniper Bluff was for my brother's wedding," Brooke was saying. She looked up as Diana stopped at their table with a coffee carafe. "And here's my amazing sister-in-law now."

Arching a brow, Diana topped off their mugs. "Don't tell me I'm the subject of more town gossip?"

Shaun did a double take. "So you two are related?"

"We were best friends in college and I introduced her to my big brother. Long story." Brooke gave a meaningful eye roll. "But finally, all these years later, they're back together and happily married."

Guess Shaun still had a few local connections to work out. Except for running the occasional errand for Kent or grabbing a quick cup of coffee at Diana's Donuts, he spent most of his time at the ranch. Keeping a low profile meant less explaining to do, and more time to think and pray.

He took another gulp of coffee before pushing his chair back. "I should get going. Got a pickup-load of supplies Kent's waiting on. Nice meeting you, Brooke. And thanks for letting me share your table."

"Actually, I think it was the other way around, but thank you, too." Her perky smile practically lit up the room, and Shaun almost felt sorry he wouldn't have a chance to get to know her better.

Which was crazy because clearly they traveled in different circles. More accurately, Shaun was currently caught in a going-nowhere loop, whereas Brooke Willoughby zipped along on the straight and narrow road to success.

Frowning, Brooke watched Shaun amble out of the doughnut shop. In her advertising work she'd had a lot of practice reading people, but he defied her powers of perception.

After offering refills to the customers at the next table, Diana plopped down in the chair Shaun had vacated. "He's a puzzle, isn't he?"

Brooke jerked her head around. "Who—the guy who was just here?"

"Don't pretend you aren't curious. We all are." Gripping the edge of the table, Diana leaned forward. "So, what did y'all talk about? Did he reveal any interesting details about himself?"

"I think I did most of the talking—as usual." Brooke lifted her coffee mug only to decide she'd had enough caffeine already. She set it down with a thunk. "All he basically said was that he hadn't been in town very long—"

"And he's staying with his almost-brother-in-law until after the wedding. Yada yada." Diana crossed her arms and leaned back. "I was hoping for something a little juicier."

"Digging for new gossip? Girl, you've been in the coffee-and-doughnuts business way too long." Mimicking her sister-in-law's pose, Brooke smirked and shook her head. "Anyway, I just met the guy. I should be asking you the questions. Who's his sister? Anyone I've met?"

"Erin Dearborn. She's Wanda Flynn's partner at the WE Design shop across the square."

"Oh, of course. Erin's living in your old house, right?" Brooke tapped both temples in a *duh* gesture. "I may never get used to how in a small town everybody knows everybody."

Diana's expression turned sympathetic. "After living in LA, this has to be a huge change. Think you'll adjust?"

"I'm sure I will...in time." She certainly hoped so, since she hadn't had much choice in the matter. "Anyway, Dad loves it here, and that's what counts."

"It was definitely a blessing when the chamber of commerce position opened up. We knew you'd be the perfect candidate."

"Which reminds me," Brooke said, collecting her shoulder bag, "I need to review my notes one more time before this meeting. Better get to the office."

Diana walked her to the door. "Just remember, all work and no play—"

"Stop right there. I don't need both you and my big brother ganging up on me. Dad, too, for that matter. I can't believe you've already coerced me into joining a church committee."

"What better way to get plugged into your new hometown? And perfect timing, too. The committee should be gearing up for their annual Christmas outreach. You'll have a blast working with Emily Ingram, and you'll make some wonderful new friends, I promise."

"And *I* promise, there'll be plenty of time for a social life after I've settled into my new job." Stepping onto the sidewalk, Brooke scrunched her shoulders, as much from the unwelcome reminder of the approaching holidays as from the October chill in the air. She turned to Diana for a quick goodbye hug. "Gotta run. See you in church tomorrow."

Though she didn't relish getting involved with a Christmas outreach project, she couldn't help appreciating the warm and welcoming church family at Shepherd of the Hills. Just as she'd hoped, they'd already made her dad feel at home, inviting him to join the seniors group and getting him involved in all kinds of fun activities.

Fun. Brooke had all but forgotten what the word meant. Helping to care for her mother during the last couple of years of her life, trying to keep Dad's spirits up, fretting over her brother's recurring issues with Crohn's disease, all while succeeding at her high-pressure LA advertising job—no wonder her family continually nagged her to slow down and take care of herself for a change.

And she would, eventually. For now, though, staying as busy as possible was her saving grace. Besides, she thrived on exactly the kind of duties her new position entailed. She loved working with people, she loved designing effective media content and she loved the challenges of project management.

But one huge difference from the LA advertising firm? Her job at the Juniper Bluff Chamber of Commerce meant she'd be dealing with neighbors and friends, the same folks she might run into any day of the week at the supermarket, the coffee shop or at church. Her new boss was already stressing to her the importance—more accurately, the *necessity*—of community involvement. After years of intentionally keeping her professional and personal lives separate, this new way of operating would take some getting used to.

No doubt about it, her first official meeting with the board of directors had her on edge. She might already have the job, but she needed to assure the local business community of her dedication and enthusiasm. A quick perusal of her skirt convinced her the coffee mishap was barely noticeable. With a confidence-boosting inhalation, she checked traffic before crossing First Street.

Following a path through the town square, she nodded politely to other townsfolk enjoying the brisk, sunny day—families walking their dogs, children playing tag, a romantic couple gazing into each other's eyes across a picnic table. On her left, Brooke passed the commemorative statue of Jake Austin, a town hero who'd died while rescuing a family from a car accident. Down another path to the right stood the gazebo, where a local country band entertained a small but growing crowd who clapped to the beat and sang along.

Small-town life. Brooke paused to soak it in. If she tried really hard to make this work, maybe she *could* be happy here. And perhaps, in time, the weight of the past few years would begin to slide off her shoulders.

Yes. Yes, I can do this. A determined smile forming, she continued across the square.

As she neared Main Street, someone seated on a park bench stood abruptly. When she sidestepped to avoid the man, her heel caught in the grass, and she scrambled to keep from toppling.

A steadying hand gripped her forearm. "Easy there. You okay?"

"Yes, thanks." She looked up into a familiar face, with eyes as dark and brooding as a stormy sky—the same blue-gray eyes that had so recently intrigued her across the coffee shop table. Regaining her footing, she caught the strap of her purse before it slipped off her shoulder. "Shaun, right? Hi again. I'm having an unusually klutzy day, apparently."

"Entirely my fault." With his free hand, he stuffed his cell phone into his jeans pocket. His furrowed brow and sideways glance suggested his thoughts lingered elsewhere—possibly on a worrisome phone call?

Brooke could easily see why Diana and others might be curious about this mystery man. If Shaun O'Grady wasn't a rancher, then what did he do for a living? And what profession allowed a guy to take several weeks off so he could hang out with his future brother-in-law until his sister got married?

And since not a single one of these questions was any of her business, she bit her tongue and asked instead, "Weren't you in a hurry to deliver those supplies?"

"I was. I mean, I am." Shaun released a tense half chuckle. "And you've got that meeting."

"Right. So I suppose we should both be on our way."

Neither of them moved.

Then they both moved at the same time and ended up doing an awkward dance in the middle of the path.

Laughing, Brooke held up both hands. "Hold on, okay? I'll go right, you go left."

Shaun shuffled from one foot to the other. "Wait— my left, or your left?"

"Um, my left. I *think*."

A grin spread across Shaun's face, the glint of sun in his eyes turning them more blue than gray. He took both her hands. "I think I've got this. Just follow my lead." Taking two giant steps to his right, he moved her in a counterclockwise quarter-circle. "There. Now we're both headed in the right direction again."

Fingertips tingling, Brooke freed her hands. She nodded toward the curb. "And I'm guessing that's your truck over there with all the fencing stuff in the back?"

"My future brother-in-law's, actually. But yeah." Looking slightly discomfited, Shaun ran a hand across the curling brown hair at his nape. "Nice running into you again, Miss Willoughby. Hope your meeting goes well."

"Thanks. Have fun playing rancher, Mr. O'Grady."

While Shaun jogged toward his pickup, Brooke continued to the end of the block and crossed Main Street. As she pushed open the chamber office door, Shaun drove by on his way around the square. He waved, and she waved back, then shook her head as she stepped into the lobby. The man had definitely piqued her curiosity, and he was certainly easy on the eyes. But since it didn't sound like he planned on being in Juniper Bluff much longer, she'd do well to put him out of her mind and focus on impressing the board members with everything she hoped to accomplish as the chamber's new communications manager.

* * *

On the drive back to the ranch, Shaun turned up the radio full blast. Kent's preference for twangy country music didn't exactly appeal, but maybe it would help get his mind off the unsettling morning he'd just been through. If his introduction to Brooke Willoughby hadn't been plenty to shake him up, the phone call from missions director Henry Voss more than made up for it.

"We need you back in Jordan, Shaun," Henry had said. He'd gone on to describe a position overseeing a newly formed network of house churches in Amman. "You're my number one choice, but I need your answer pretty quick."

Shaun didn't feel anywhere near ready to return to full-time service. "I don't know, Henry. I'm still figuring things out."

"I understand. Take a couple of weeks to think it over and pray about it. I know God will lead you in the right direction."

He only wished he shared Henry's confidence—not in God's wisdom but in his own ability to discern the Lord's leading.

Or could this position be God's answer to Shaun's confusion? Maybe God just needed him to release his faith struggles and simply trust again. All he had to do was call the director back and say yes.

After parking the pickup next to the barn, he opened the recent calls list on his phone, his thumb hovering over Henry's name. But the pinch in his gut wouldn't let him complete the call. Barging from the truck, he stuffed the phone in his pocket. All he wanted right now was to lose himself in the monotony of helping Kent plant fence posts.

So he threw himself into that task, losing track of the time as the relentless work cleared his mind. By early afternoon, they'd set up temporary fencing through a section of pasture and connected the wire to a solar-powered charger. Afterward, Shaun moved out of the way while Kent climbed on Jasmine, his big black cutting horse, to herd several head of cattle into the fenced-off section. Kent said rotating grazing areas helped maintain the ecology of the land. Or something like that. All Shaun knew was that he'd worked up enough of a sweat stomping fence posts into the ground that he no longer needed his quilted flannel jacket.

With the task complete, he waded through knee-high grass and weeds to where he'd parked the pickup on a narrow rutted lane. A few minutes later, he caught up with Kent at the barn. Going cross-country on Jasmine, Kent had made better time and probably enjoyed a smoother ride as well. Bouncing over all those rocks and potholes had been painfully reminiscent of Shaun's most recent missionary years in Ethiopia. His tailbone still ached at the memory of driving an ancient Land Rover with no shocks over roads better suited for donkeys and goats. Jordan, on the other hand, held much more pleasant memories…but was that incentive enough?

Pocketing the truck keys, he clamped his teeth together. Henry had given him two weeks. If God hadn't given him a crystal clear no by then, he'd accept the call and start making plans for his return to Jordan, a previous post where he'd felt he really had made a difference. With that much settled for now, he put Henry's call out of his mind and focused on the task at hand.

While Kent tended to Jasmine, Shaun unloaded the pickup bed and stowed the leftover wire and fence posts in the storage room. As he finished, his sister's car pulled up outside the barn. He strode out to meet her and was nearly bowled over when Avery, his seven-year-old niece, plowed into him.

"Uncle Shaun, look! I lost another tooth." Avery tipped her head back and opened her mouth.

"Whoa, you sure did. Hope the tooth fairy was generous." He dropped to one knee to inspect the newly vacant spot on her upper gum. The shiny serrated edge of a new tooth already peeked through.

Avery cupped her hand around Shaun's ear. "It's okay. I know Mom's really the tooth fairy. And she gave me two whole quarters."

"Cool. Don't spend it all in one place." Tousling his niece's mop of pale red curls, Shaun pushed to his feet. "Hey, Erin. Back for more wedding planning?"

"If I can tear my cowboy away from his cows. Looks like y'all have been working hard today." Erin wrinkled her nose as she came closer. "Smells like it, too. Watch out, or Kent will make a rancher of you yet."

"Don't hold your breath." Then Shaun got a whiff of himself. "On second thought, maybe you should, at least until I get cleaned up."

They all entered the farmhouse, and Shaun made quick work of going to his room, discarding his soiled clothes and washing up.

By the time Shaun came downstairs in a fresh polo shirt and jeans, Kent had already cleaned up, too. He and Erin had just sat down at the kitchen table with glasses of iced tea and their wedding planning notebook.

Kent motioned Shaun over. "Pour yourself some tea and join us. I'm supposed to be picking a groom's cake and I need another male's perspective."

"Afraid I wouldn't be much help in the cake depart-
ment. Think I'll see what Avery's watching on TV."
Shaun started for the living room.

"Uh-uh, big brother." Erin patted the chair next to
her. "Sit down a minute. There's something else we've
been meaning to ask you."

Erin's elfin smile belied the hint of something more
serious in her tone. Figuring this didn't involve cake selections, Shaun cautiously lowered himself into the chair.
"I'm not the guy to give advice about tuxes or flowers
either, in case you were wondering."

"Actually…" Erin reached for her fiancé's hand, and
Kent scooted closer. They both looked slightly nervous.
"What we wanted to ask—I mean, with you being an or-
dained minister—"

Palms outward, he leaned back in the chair. "I think
I know where this is going, and the answer is no."

"But it would mean so much to have my brother officiate at our wedding. Please, Shaun, would you at least
think about it?"

"I'm honored and touched that you would ask, but I'm
not ready to—" His mouth went dry. He couldn't meet
his sister's gaze. "Sorry, I just can't do it." He shoved up
from the table and marched upstairs.

Alone in the guest room, he sank onto the bed and
dropped his head into his hands. Didn't they understand
how messed up he was? When he couldn't even discern
God's will for his own life, what made them think he
could bestow a proper blessing on their marriage? After
all his sister had been through with her abusive first husband and starting over after their divorce, she deserved
only the best.

It was Greg, the eldest of the O'Grady siblings, who'd

had the bright idea Shaun should spend some time in Juniper Bluff after returning from his most recent—and most discouraging—missionary assignment. This was supposed to be a kind of sabbatical, reconnecting with himself and with God. So far, all he had to show for it was more confusion, along with several new calluses from the hard labor of ranch work.

He wished he had the sense of direction of the woman he'd met this morning—Brooke Willoughby. An image of her crept into his thoughts. There was a woman who knew where she was going. She might display a few nervous twinges about settling into her new job, but underneath it all she exuded professionalism and self-assurance. True, he couldn't deny the irrational spark of attraction he'd felt, but besides the fact that they were both new in town, what could they possibly have in common?

Not that it mattered, since their paths weren't likely to cross again anytime soon.

Then why, absurdly, did he wish somehow they would?

Chapter Two

Leaving the sanctuary with Kent, Erin and Avery after worship on Sunday morning, Shaun glimpsed a familiar cascade of honey-brown curls. So much for discounting his chances of running into Brooke Willoughby. This was small-town Juniper Bluff, after all. Engaged in a spirited conversation with Diana from the doughnut shop and another woman, she didn't notice him as he walked past.

"That's the new communications manager for the chamber," Erin said. "I met her in the women's Bible study this morning. She's really on the ball."

"Yeah, I know." As they continued toward the exit, Shaun couldn't keep his head from swiveling in Brooke's direction.

Erin looked at him askance. "You *know*?"

Shaun should have kept his mouth shut. He faced forward and walked faster. "Diana's Donuts was packed yesterday, so we shared a table."

A mischievous chuckle erupted from Erin's throat. "Kent needs to send you to town more often."

"Speaking of which," Kent said, tapping his church

bulletin against his palm, "I've been working on getting more connected here at church, and the service committee looks interesting. They're meeting tomorrow night to discuss plans for this year's Christmas charity project. Why don't you tag along with me?"

Shaun gave his head a brisk shake. "I don't think so."

"Come on, it'll do you good to get out and meet more people." They'd reached Erin's car, and Kent helped Avery buckle into the back seat. Blocking Shaun from proceeding on toward the pickup, he glowered. "How long have you been staying with me at the ranch now—a month? Six weeks? About all you come to town for is to pick up something for me at the ranch supply store or to visit Erin at her place."

"I've been attending church with you nearly every Sunday," Shaun shot back. "And didn't I just say I met Brooke at the doughnut shop? So I get out plenty. I've got all the acquaintances I need."

Kent shared a meaningful look with Erin, and then both of them pinned him with concerned frowns. "I spent years holding things in," Kent said quietly, "isolating myself when I could have been sharing my problems with people who cared. So I know avoidance when I see it."

Hands on hips, Shaun exhaled sharply through his nose. Erin and Kent had been more than patient with him as he worked through his issues with God. He knew they were only trying to help. "Okay, you could have a point. But these past few years trying to make a difference in Ethiopia… I can't begin to describe the frustration and disappointment."

"We know, Shaun." Erin touched his arm. "And we understand why you needed to get away and decompress. But getting involved in something on a smaller scale—a project where you can readily see the results of your efforts—might turn out to be just what you need."

Shaun didn't want to admit it, but his sister could be right. "All right," he said, hands raised. "No promises, but I'll attend the meeting with you and see what it's all about."

Kent clapped him on the shoulder. "Good man. Now, let's go see what Erin's got cookin' for dinner."

One thing Shaun had learned upon his arrival in Juniper Bluff was that his little sister had become not only a talented interior designer but a pretty amazing cook. He'd come to look forward to meals at her house or when she brought something special out to Kent's.

He was proud of his baby sister in other ways, too, and felt rotten that while serving overseas he'd been unaware of everything she'd gone through with her abusive first husband. It helped only slightly to know their older brother, Greg, hadn't been any more clued in than Shaun. Until the bitter end, Erin had managed to hide the truth from almost everyone close to her. Guess it ran in the family.

Interesting how Greg had contrived to send both his troubled siblings to Juniper Bluff to heal and start over. Erin had found not only a profitable outlet for her design talents but true love with someone who'd treat her right. Shaun had no expectations of romance, but if his sojourn in this friendly small town made room for God to shed a little light on his path, he'd be grateful.

He chuckled to himself as he wondered when his philanthropic elder brother would leave big-city San Antonio behind and settle in Juniper Bluff permanently. Greg spent a good part of his time here anyway to oversee the Camp Serenity program for disadvantaged kids at Serenity Hills Guest Ranch. It was probably only a matter of time before Greg started pestering Shaun to join him as a volunteer counselor, but that sounded too long-term.

On the other hand, the Christmas outreach project had a clear beginning and end, which seemed much more doable, something Shaun could complete even if he did feel led to accept the Jordan position.

On Monday evening he rode into town with Kent for the meeting. Erin wouldn't be participating—too many wedding details to iron out, Kent explained, plus she stayed busy with her interior design clients and keeping up with Avery.

They arrived at the church a few minutes early, and Kent introduced Shaun to the chairperson, Emily Ingram. "Emily's married to Dr. Robert Ingram, the vet who takes care of my livestock."

Shaun smiled and offered his hand. He recognized Emily as the woman Brooke Willoughby had been in conversation with yesterday after church.

"A missionary *and* a minister," Emily gushed. "I know you'll be a huge asset to the group."

He suffered a moment of regret for not asking Kent to omit that part of his background. "Just consider me another willing worker."

As other committee members trickled in, Shaun took a seat next to Kent near the end of a long, oval conference table. Clearing her throat, Emily Ingram prepared to open the meeting, only to pause at the click of heels in the corridor.

Seconds later, Brooke Willoughby slipped into the room. She offered a shy smile. "Hope I'm not late."

"Just getting started, Brooke. Have a seat." Emily motioned toward the only empty chair, directly across from Shaun. While Brooke got situated, Emily introduced her. "Many of you know Brooke's brother, Tripp, Robert's partner at the vet clinic. Brooke just accepted a position at the chamber of commerce, and we're delighted to welcome her to Juniper Bluff."

Brooke's cheeks colored at the polite smattering of applause. "Thanks. I'm looking forward to getting to know everyone." Then her gaze met Shaun's, and a surprised glint flickered in her brown eyes. "Oh. Hi."

He couldn't explain the flutter beneath his sternum. For one thing, he wasn't the type to experience flutters in the presence of an attractive woman. For another, he'd already surmised their strongest common link was an affinity for good coffee.

Calling the meeting to order, Emily saved him from having to form a coherent response. After opening with a brief prayer, she consulted her printed agenda. "In the interest of time, I'd like to table the usual reports until the end and get right to our Christmas service project." When no one objected, she went on, "Since this is my first year to chair the committee, I did a little research to see what's been done in the past—helping a needy family buy gifts for their children, serving Christmas dinner at a shelter, and I think last year you put together care packages for the Camp Serenity kids."

Shaun sat back and listened while the committee batted around those ideas and a few others. After several minutes, he glanced across the table to see Brooke silently chewing her lip and added one more thing to their list of commonalities. As the two newbies on the committee, both were reluctant to wade into the middle of a discussion that grew more vocal as each new idea emerged.

Emily tapped the table with her pen. "With so many

possibilities to consider, I suggest we give oversight of the project to one or two individuals. They can sort through the options, make the final decision and then get back to the committee with their directives for implementation."

At last, a voice of reason. Shaun liked Emily Ingram already. He scanned the room and tried to guess which among the regulars would get the chairperson's nod. Probably not Kent, since he was in the middle of planning a wedding. Maybe the sixty-ish lady at the other end of the table who'd had plenty to say about nearly every idea presented?

Then he felt Emily's gaze on him. She smiled like the proverbial cat who ate the canary. "Nothing compares with the freshness of new ways of looking at things. Shaun and Brooke, our newest committee members, could we prevail upon the two of you to head up our Christmas outreach efforts?"

Brooke's gaze locked with Shaun's. Squirming in his chair, he looked equally taken aback by Emily's request. Brooke forced down a swallow while pawing through her oversize purse for the water bottle she'd brought. She'd tried to persuade both Diana and Emily yesterday that she wasn't quite ready for committee involvement, but she may as well have been arguing with those fence posts Shaun had been hauling. Maybe if she stalled long enough, he'd make convincing excuses for both of them.

He coughed into his fist. "I actually just came along at Kent's invitation. I'm not really in a position to—"

"Oh, you'll do fine." Emily reached across the table to pat his wrist, then did the same to Brooke. "With your unique combination of skills and experience, you two are exactly what this committee needs."

Nearly choking on a sip of water, Brooke shook her head. "Wouldn't you rather ask someone who knows the community much better than either of us?"

"Right," Shaun agreed. "We're both practically strangers to Juniper Bluff." He set his hands on the armrests as if preparing for a quick exit.

Kent, obviously the future brother-in-law Shaun had mentioned, chuckled to himself while appearing a teensy bit remorseful about setting Shaun up for this. Family pressure? Brooke could totally relate.

Emily maintained her ethereal smile as she jotted notes. "Shaun and Brooke, why don't you two get together over the next couple of weeks and hammer out a plan of action? You can report back to us at our next meeting."

Brooke cast Shaun a get-us-out-of-this stare. He responded with tight lips and a helpless shrug. Before either of them had a chance for further protests, Emily moved on to the next item on the agenda. Brooke scarcely heard a word as she mentally rehearsed one statement after another about why she was a bad choice for this assignment. She'd hit Emily with them the moment the meeting ended. The glazed look in Shaun's eyes suggested he was doing exactly the same.

After other business had been covered and Emily adjourned the meeting, Brooke and Shaun attempted to corner her. The woman barely slowed her pace as she turned off lights, locked the classroom and marched out to the parking lot. But no matter how forcefully they reiterated their objections, she insisted they were more than up for the task and they should feel free to call if they had any questions.

"Oh, boy, I've got plenty," Brooke muttered as Emily drove away.

Shaun stood beside her. "Remind me to strangle my almost-brother-in-law."

"Where is he, by the way?"

"Over there waiting for me in his truck." Shaun nodded toward the dusty tan pickup Brooke had seen him driving on Saturday. "Kent should have warned me. His prize Brangus bull's got nothing on the world's most ruthless committee chairperson."

Giving a snort, Brooke rifled through her purse for her keys. "I definitely need to have a word with my brother and sister-in-law."

"Don't tell me—you were steamrolled into joining the committee, too?"

"My family seems to think I need an actual life away from the office." Brooke rolled her eyes. "Bossy big brothers and their wives are the worst."

"Meddlesome little sisters and their fiancés are just as bad." Shaun took a few steps toward Kent's pickup, then turned and blew out a resigned sigh. "So, I guess we're doing this?"

"If for no other reason than to prove Emily wrong. Should we decide on a time to talk one day soon?"

Offering a wry half smile, Shaun said, "I'm not the one keeping office hours. You name the time and place."

"Things are a little crazy at the chamber right now while I get a handle on this new job. But maybe we could meet early one morning for coffee."

"That works. Anyway, I'd say Diana owes you free coffee and doughnuts for life."

Brooke snickered. "I'd have to agree." She took out her cell phone and they traded numbers. "I'll give you a call after I double-check my calendar at the office tomorrow."

They said good-night, and Brooke slid behind the wheel of her metallic-red sedan. Passing the town square on her way home, she recalled her first two encounters with Shaun O'Grady. She still didn't know what to make of the man. Although, thanks to Emily's brief introductions of the other committee members, Brooke now knew Shaun was an ordained minister and former missionary—both of which made him much more qualified for a church outreach project. Maybe she could plead busyness and convince him to take the lead.

Besides, she'd been sorely dreading Christmas, her second since Mom died. Last year, she and Dad had been able to distract themselves with excitement over Tripp and Diana's January wedding. This season, Brooke had planned to stay so busy at the chamber that she wouldn't have time to think about the approaching holidays.

So much for that idea. At this rate, Christmas could be at the top of her priority list for weeks to come.

A few minutes later, she parked in the garage at home. She and her dad had rented a two-bedroom brick cottage down the block from Tripp and Diana's house. For her dad's sake, she couldn't deny the advantages of living near family again, but being this close would take some getting used to. Especially if they insisted on micromanaging her personal life.

"How was the meeting?" Dad asked as she let herself in through the kitchen. He'd just poured himself a bowl of oat cereal as a bedtime snack.

Brooke tossed her purse onto a chair. "Fine, if you count getting roped into cochairing the Christmas outreach subcommittee. Tripp and Diana are *so* going to pay for this."

Dad merely chuckled. "Not biting off more than you can chew, are you?"

"Probably." After filling a cereal bowl for herself, Brooke plopped down at the table across from her father. "Hopefully my new partner in crime will carry most of the load."

"And who might that be?"

"Guess I didn't tell you about the guy I met at the coffee shop on Saturday. His name's Shaun O'Grady, also new in town. He's a minister taking a break from missionary work. That's about the extent of what I know about him."

"Old, young?" Dad swallowed a spoonful of cereal, then winked. "Married, single?"

Making a growling sound in her throat, Brooke glanced toward the ceiling. "Probably around my age and probably single. Happy now?"

"I'm plenty happy. The question is, are *you*?"

She let her father's words hang in the air while she finished her cereal. But the question followed her even as she changed into her pajamas and crawled into bed. No doubt about it, the last couple of years had taken a toll, both emotionally and physically. Add her nonexistent romantic life into the mix and things looked even drearier. The life she'd always striven to keep perfectly under control had disintegrated beneath her. No matter how hard she tried to ignore it, the nagging sense of failure lingered.

Not even the move to Juniper Bluff had been entirely in her control. Struggling through her grief over Mom's death, she'd had no other goal than to bolster her advertising clientele and strengthen her position at the advertising firm. Little did she realize her family had been working behind the scenes to bring her and Dad back to Texas.

Okay, yes, seeing Dad happier than he'd been since Mom had first developed kidney disease was definitely a blessing.

But being strong-armed into working with an almost-complete stranger on a project she had neither the time nor the experience for? This was a situation she needed to get under control ASAP.

After returning calls and replying to a few emails Tuesday morning, Brooke decided she couldn't put off the inevitable. She found Shaun's number in her phone and pressed the call button.

He answered with a breathy "Hello?"

"Hi, it's Brooke. Is this a bad time?"

"Just caught me hauling a hay bale, one of the many delightful ranch chores I've been delegated."

She chuckled. "I take it your future brother-in-law is still alive and kicking."

"Yeah, my sister's put a lot of effort into planning the wedding, so she'd be really miffed if I did him in."

"Oh, the sacrifices we make for family." *No kidding.* "So, about this Christmas project…"

"Right. Unless you've come up with a brilliant idea to get us out of it, we should probably start brainstorming."

Brooke perused her computer calendar. "Shall we meet at the doughnut shop for coffee in the morning, say around seven—or is that too early for you?"

"I'm an early riser, or at least I've become one since moving in with Kent. See you then."

Ending the call, Brooke typed in the appointment. A moment later, Inez Quick, the chamber president, tapped on Brooke's open door. She carried an armful of file folders.

Brooke gave a mock groan. "More stuff I need to familiarize myself with?"

"No rush." The slender fifty-something woman dropped the stack on Brooke's desk, then tucked a strand of dark hair into her French twist. "These contain minutes and project reports from several of our committees. Speaking of which, how did your church meeting go last night?"

"Can you spell *gullible*? Seems the newest kids on the block are prime targets for getting volunteered." She went on to explain about the Christmas outreach.

With a thoughtful smile, Inez perched on a chair across from Brooke. "Think of it this way. The more in tune you are with the pulse of Juniper Bluff, the more effective you'll be at this job."

Loath as she was to admit it, her boss had a point. At least it was easier to swallow than her family's constant harassment about getting a life. "Problem is, I'm so new in town that I have no idea where to begin."

Inez reached across the desk for a pen and scratchpad. After jotting some notes, she passed it back to Brooke. "Here's a list off the top of my head of area agencies that support needy families. Contact a few of them and ask for ways your committee might help."

Brooke perused the list. "Thanks, this is great."

Rising, Inez turned to go. "Oh, and feel free to work on the project during office hours as your schedule permits. I meant what I said—this could help you build a few more inroads with the local business community."

Having her boss's approval alleviated a few of her concerns about spending time on the project. By the end of the day she'd called every organization on Inez's list and had also contacted Pastor Terry at Shepherd of the Hills to ask about any particular needs he might be aware of. The responses she'd collected would give her and Shaun more than enough to kick off their planning session. The hard part would be narrowing down the options to what would best fit the abilities and interests of the service committee.

Armed with computer notes full of information from the agencies she'd called, Brooke arrived at Diana's Donuts the next morning a few minutes before seven. She was surprised to find Shaun already holding a table for them.

"You really are an early bird," she said as she set down her things.

Shaun smiled over the rim of his coffee mug. "Didn't want to hold you up in case you were in a hurry to get to work."

"No worries. I now officially have my boss's go-ahead for this venture, which means we won't have to meet at zero dark thirty next time." She covered a yawn. "Be right back after I get some coffee."

Diana greeted her at the counter. "Conspiring with the handsome new stranger, I see."

"Conspiring—really?" Brooke rolled her eyes. Safer not to acknowledge the *handsome new stranger* remark at all—not that she hadn't noticed. In fact, the more Shaun's beard grew out, the more her gaze drifted to his manly chin. "We're just working together on this church outreach thing."

"So your dad told me when he and Tripp dropped by here yesterday." Diana passed Brooke a mug of steaming coffee, then leaned closer, elbows resting on the counter.

"I hear he's a pastor who's been serving on the mission field. What else have you found out about him?"

"Honestly, you never used to be this gossipy in college." Lifting her mug, Brooke offered a sugary-sweet smile. "On the house, right? Thank you so much." She ignored Diana's raised-eyebrow stare and sauntered back to the table.

Shaun seemed to come out of a daze as she sat down across from him. Straightening, he offered a brief smile. "Ready to get down to business?"

Brooke studied him. "Your heart still isn't in this, is it?"

"Let's just say I'm continuing to reserve judgment."

"Believe me, I understand." Maybe if she focused less on the Christmas angle and more on the community service aspects, it would be easier to detach from her emotions.

Shaun released a resigned sigh. "I did jot down a few thoughts, though."

"Good. We can combine your ideas with what I've gleaned from area aid organizations." *Yes, let's keep this all business.* She reached into her tote for her tablet computer. Tapping a few icons, she brought up her notes from yesterday's calls.

"Wow, high-tech." With a wry laugh, Shaun tugged a folded paper from the pocket of his plaid flannel shirt. "Hope my handwritten jottings aren't too old-school for you."

"As long as your hen-scratching is decipherable, I'm good."

Shaun's eyes narrowed in feigned offense. "My penmanship is excellent, and I can produce my third-grade report card to prove it."

Every time a touch of the man's humor rose to the surface made it easier to like him. Maybe they could actually make this work. Wiggling a brow, she held out her hand for the paper. "I prefer to judge for myself, if you don't mind."

He slapped it into her palm, then sat back and smugly crossed his arms.

"Hmm, yes, a graceful slant, nicely rounded letters, clean and confident lines. Quite passable. Well done, Mr. O'Grady." Her teasing expression turned apologetic. "Excuse me. I guess that should be Reverend O'Grady. I didn't know until the meeting that you're a minister."

Shaun glanced away, his jaw clenched. "Wish Emily hadn't said anything."

"I'm sorry," Brooke murmured, concerned she'd somehow offended him. "I didn't realize you wanted to keep it private."

"It's not that so much." Drawing a deep breath, Shaun folded his hands on the table. "But people respond to clergy a little differently, and since I didn't come to Juniper Bluff for anything more than some much needed R and R, I don't advertise my professional background."

Brooke nodded. "That helps me understand your reluctance to get involved in this service project. If you really don't want to do it—"

He interrupted her with a weak laugh. "Hey, if it'll give me a break from mucking stalls and hauling hay bales, I'm in. So let's hash out some ideas, okay?"

They spent the next half hour comparing notes and listing the pros and cons of various service possibilities. Brooke quickly discovered they were coming at the project from two very different perspectives—hers shaped by results-oriented efficiency, while Shaun leaned toward the personal aspects. By the time Brooke had to leave for the office, they'd whittled the list down to the top three service projects they could agree on.

"Let's think on these and meet again in a few days," she suggested. "I'll do more research, too."

Shaun fingered his empty coffee mug, his brows converging to form a pensive crease down the middle of his forehead. "You know, there's one thing we haven't done yet, and I'm embarrassed for not suggesting it."

Brooke looked up from tucking her tablet into her tote. "Oh? What have I missed?"

"We haven't prayed about what we're doing."

Now Brooke was embarrassed, and more than a little ashamed of how her mother's lengthy illness and death had slowly eroded her prayer life. "You're right. I can get so focused on the details that I forget to bring God in."

"But I've got no excuse." Shaun's mouth twisted in a pained smile, and he lowered his voice. "I'm a pastor, remember?"

The resignation in his blue-gray stare shifted something in Brooke's heart. Diana was right—there was much more to Shaun O'Grady than met the eye. "Would you like to say a prayer now?"

Shaun bowed his head, and Brooke did the same. "Lord, we're two newcomers to this town and church, but for whatever reason, we've been called upon to serve. Guide us and help us to do our best for You and for those who will be blessed by our efforts. In Your Son's name, amen."

"Thank you," Brooke said, a catch in her voice. "Remind me to have you pray at each of our meetings."

"We could take turns, you know."

"Uh, no, that's okay. You're the pro in the prayer de-partment." With a quick breath, she stood and slid the strap of her tote to her shoulder.

Walking out together, they agreed to meet again on Saturday, and Brooke hurried across the square to the chamber office. There, at least, she could pretend for a while that she had everything under control.

Chapter Three

The next few days had Shaun overanalyzing everything about Wednesday's meeting with Brooke—including his openness to pray. Proved he and God were still on speaking terms, anyway, even if he was still light-years away from discerning the Lord's plan for his life.

Walking one of Kent's horses out to pasture on Saturday morning, he gave the gentle sorrel mare a scratch under the chin. Posey snorted her appreciation, her warm breath forming clouds in the chilly air. "You've got it good here, girl," Shaun said as he unbuckled her halter. "Maybe if I spent my days munching grass and rolling in the dust, life wouldn't seem so complicated."

"Talking to horses is good therapy."

Shaun turned to find Kent grinning at him across the fence rail. "One thing's for sure—they don't give me grief like my future brother-in-law."

Kent released the gate latch and waited for Shaun to amble out. "Thought you were meeting with Brooke again today."

"We're having an early lunch at the supermarket deli."

He looped the halter and lead rope over the rail. "Which means I need to finish my chores pretty quick and clean up."

"Work any harder around here and I won't know what to do after you move on."

Laughing, Shaun started back to the barn. "Maybe hire someone you'll actually pay?"

"Room and board's not enough for you?" Kent gave him a playful slug in the arm. "If you're holding out for cable TV and maid service, you're gonna be disappointed."

They traded a few more friendly gibes before Kent saddled Jasmine and rode out to check on his cattle, and Shaun got busy mucking stalls.

He'd enjoyed getting to know Kent over the past few weeks. Watching him with Erin evoked not only joy at seeing his sister so happy after her failed first marriage but a twinge of envy as well. Serving on the mission field, Shaun had encountered more than a few single women his age who shared both his faith and his passion for those in need. He'd even had a couple of relationships he thought might actually go somewhere.

But something always held him back. In one case, it was because he'd felt the call to transfer elsewhere, but she hadn't sensed the same leading. His second time around, they ultimately agreed their personality differences would only lead to problems down the road. But a huge factor for Shaun was the fear of divided loyalties. Could he sustain a healthy marriage while also devoting himself to mission service? And what of children? Starting a family involved a whole different set of decisions.

Now here he was, ankle-deep in soiled shavings and doing nothing remotely close to the plans and goals he'd set for himself as a seminary student. Was that the root of his current dissatisfaction—that he'd rushed ahead with his own agenda instead of listening more closely for God's direction?

He couldn't deny he'd experienced a sense of peace and relief when he'd first returned to the States and Greg had suggested he spend some time in Juniper Bluff. So maybe his stay here—yes, even the Christmas outreach project—was part of God's will.

As for meeting Brooke Willoughby? Guess he'd have to wait and see.

Two hours later, he climbed into the battered green hatchback he'd held onto since college, mainly so he'd have something to drive during his stateside visits. Arriving at the deli, he claimed a table to wait for Brooke. When she sauntered in, curls loose about her shoulders and wearing a tunic-length striped sweater over black leggings, he allowed himself an appreciative grin. Working on this project with someone as sharp *and* as pretty as Brooke Willoughby definitely earned a mark in the plus column.

Pulling out the chair across from him, she nodded as he stood to welcome her. "I like a guy who's prompt."

"Don't get used to it. A fresh deli sandwich just sounded a lot more appealing than another PB and J with Kent."

Brooke laughed as she set her tote next to her chair. "Can't blame you. Shall we talk first or get some lunch?"

"Breakfast was a long time ago. I vote for lunch," Shaun said over his rumbling stomach. "Tell me what you'd like and I'll place our order."

He returned shortly with two sandwiches, potato chips and iced teas. "The one with the straw is your sweet tea," he said. "Everything else is the same."

Unwrapping her sandwich, Brooke cast him a smile. "You got the ham and Swiss on rye, too?"

"My favorite. And sour-cream-and-onion chips— missed those like crazy overseas." Shaun ripped open the bag.

"Not a fan of sweet tea, though?"

He grimaced. "Makes my mouth pucker."

Remembering his commitment to start these meetings with prayer, he offered thanks for the meal and asked the Lord to bless their discussion. Considering how long it had taken them to narrow down their top-three list the other morning, agreeing on a single best plan of action would require God's help in abundance.

They settled into comfortable silence while they ate. The way Brooke held her sandwich just so, keeping the bottom half in the wrapper so the juices didn't drip, then dabbing the corners of her lips after every bite, Shaun couldn't picture her ever being comfortable in a Third World country. And since it looked more and more like his sabbatical would be over by the end of the year, whatever other common likes or dislikes they might discover were moot.

Finishing the last bite of her sandwich, Brooke wadded up the wrapper. "Guess we should get started."

After another swig of tea, Shaun reached beneath his chair for the steno pad he'd been using to collect his thoughts.

He watched with amusement while Brooke cleared a space on the small table for her tablet computer with attached keyboard. She laid her cell phone beside it. After several keystrokes and a few scowls and *hmm*s while she appeared to search for her notes, she looked up with a satisfied smile. "Okay, all set."

With great flourish, Shaun flipped open his steno

pad and whipped a ballpoint pen from his shirt pocket. "Me, too."

Her scowl returned, but a teasing glint flashed in her eyes. "You're purposely trying to annoy me, I can tell."

"Who, me?" What was it about this woman that brought out his playful side? Or was he merely growing more and more relaxed the longer he stayed in Juniper Bluff? Either way, it was a welcome change. He sat back and crossed his arms. "Since you're so organized, why don't you go first?"

"I will, thank you." Brooke arched a brow as she turned her attention to her tablet screen. "Of the top three ideas we'd settled on, I'm leaning toward collecting grocery items and delivering them to needy families so they can make their own Christmas dinner. One of the agencies I contacted said they could provide some names."

"Christmas dinner? Is that the best we can do?" Shaun had already crossed that idea off his list. All humor evaporating, he flipped to the page where he'd jotted his reasons. "Donating a few turkeys, yams and cans of cranberry sauce sounds easy and doable. But it's one meal. So we do our good deed for the holiday and feel good about ourselves for the rest of the year, while these families face another year of wondering how they're going to feed their kids or keep a roof over their heads? Sorry, that doesn't work for me."

Brooke stiffened. "Obviously, you have strong feelings about this. I wish you'd said something before we included that option on our list."

He hadn't meant to offend her, but clearly he had. He lifted both hands in a conciliatory gesture. "I've had more time to think about it, that's all, and I think we can do better. I'd rather we choose something that will benefit the recipients for more than a single day."

Lips pursed, Brooke typed something into her tablet. "Okay, one of our other ideas was organizing a Christmas store. We talked about collecting toys, clothing and other items, and then bringing families in to select Christmas gifts for each other—things they'd be able to use *year-round*." She shot him a raised-eyebrow glare that communicated, *I dare you to shoot this one down*.

He drew a deep breath. "On the surface, it seems like a good plan. But you know what they say. Give a man a fish and he'll eat for a day—"

"Teach a man to fish and he'll never go hungry." Brooke nodded briskly. "I get it, okay? But this is *just* a Christmas outreach. That's all we signed up for. We're not out to save the world."

Fist clenched in his lap, Shaun glanced away. "*Just* doesn't cut it for me, Brooke. Never has, never will." Scooting his chair back, he gathered up his pen and steno pad along with the trash from his lunch. "Sorry to cut this short, but I told Kent I'd mow his lawn this afternoon. I should get going."

What just happened here? Brooke picked up her jaw before it crashed onto her tablet keyboard. She swiveled in time to see Shaun toss his trash into the nearest receptacle before he marched out of the deli.

"We never even got to idea number three," she muttered, her gaze shooting daggers at Shaun's rapidly retreating back. Oh, well, he probably had a dozen reasons why he didn't like that one, either.

Then why hadn't he said something the other day when they were first paring down their list?

Her glance fell upon a nearby display of baked goods, where a tin of chocolate-frosted brownies sprinkled with walnuts caught her eye. Unable to resist, she hurried to stow her tablet and dispose of her trash, then took the brownies to the deli cashier. Five minutes later, she sat in her car with the open container on her lap. She was just about frustrated enough to eat the whole batch.

Sanity prevailed, however, and she stopped at two. After finding a used tissue to wipe crumbs and frosting off her lips and fingers, she decided some retail therapy was in order. Maybe not as good for her wallet but much better for the waistline. She headed downtown and parked at one end of Main Street across from the town square.

Two ladies' boutiques, a card shop and the drugstore later, she now owned a new pair of silver hoop earrings and two bottles of nail polish. The next shop, WE Design, boasted a window display of handmade baskets amid autumn leaves and colorful gourds. While Brooke gnawed her lower lip and wondered if Shaun's sister had made these baskets, an auburn-haired woman juggling an art portfolio and a huge cardboard box stumbled toward the entrance.

"Let me get the door for you," Brooke offered, recognizing Erin Dearborn from the Sunday school class. "Looks like you've got your hands full."

"Thank you!" Sparkling blue eyes peeked over the top of the box. "It's not as heavy as it looks, just bulky."

As Brooke held the door, the petite woman edged through. A glimpse inside the crate revealed several different-sized baskets. "You're Shaun O'Grady's sister, aren't you?"

"Yes, and you're Brooke from the chamber. Hi, nice to see you again."

A million questions racing through her head, Brooke followed Erin inside. Maybe Shaun's sister could give her a little more insight into what made the guy tick.

Behind the counter, a buxom woman in a full, flowing skirt was completing a phone call. She stepped around to relieve Erin of the box. "Mrs. Yates just called to reschedule her living-room consultation for Monday morning. Said she forgot about the church seniors trip to Kerrville today."

Church seniors trip—must be the same one Brooke's dad had signed up for. Seemed his social life was going gangbusters since they moved to Juniper Bluff.

Erin set down her portfolio. "Oh, good. That gives me more time to fine-tune my presentation." She turned to Brooke with a smile. "Let me introduce Wanda Flynn, the other half of WE Design."

Wanda offered her hand. "Redecorating is our specialty. Is there a project we can help you with?"

"Actually, I was hoping Erin could spare a few minutes. I'm Brooke Willoughby. Shaun and I—"

"Yes, the church committee. I'm so glad you two are working together." Erin leaned closer, her tone becoming secretive. "He'd never admit it, but he really needs this."

Maybe so, but Brooke didn't need the man's uncompromising attitude. "Can I buy you a cup of coffee?"

Ten minutes later, they sat across from each other at Diana's Donuts. Brooke had wisely left her remaining brownies in the car, but control had gone out the window since lunch, and she couldn't resist a caramel latte with whipped cream. Watching Erin sip Earl Grey with nothing but a dash of honey, Brooke suffered a twinge of guilt but quickly brushed it aside. She had more pressing matters on her mind than counting calories.

"I assume you want to talk about my brother," Erin said with a guarded smile.

"I'm just trying to understand him." Brooke dabbed whipped cream from her lips. "We met over lunch to discuss this outreach project but couldn't agree on anything."

"I guess it's pretty obvious Shaun is an idealist, especially when it comes to making people's lives better."

"Which I'm sure served him well on the mission field. But this is small-town Juniper Bluff, and we're just one teensy church committee." Brooke's frustration boiled over again. "*Just.* That's the exact word he used. He said *just* doesn't cut it for him."

"Sounds like Shaun. He's never done anything halfway. Kent, my fiancé, even jokes about how hard Shaun works at the ranch."

Another sip of the caramel latte left a cloying taste in Brooke's mouth. She set the mug aside and folded her hands. "So how do I work with him without losing my mind? I don't want to disappoint the service committee, but if he isn't willing to bend a little, this project is dead in the water."

"I wish I had answers for you." Sighing, Erin rested her forearms on the table. "When Shaun came home from the mission field at the end of the summer, he was a real mess—angry, discouraged, totally burned out. That's why our brother Greg brought him to Juniper Bluff. We're hoping his time here will give him some perspective and help him figure out where God wants him."

So he was merely biding his time, hoping for an answer to drop out of the sky? Typically preferring action over indecisiveness, Brooke wasn't sure she could relate. She raised her hands in surrender and leaned back in her chair. "Okay, I'll try to keep an open mind. But Christmas isn't that far away, and we need to agree on a plan sooner rather than later."

"I'll try talking to him, too. Just be patient. If you're willing to give his ideas a chance, I know this will all work out for the best." With a quick glance at the time, Erin drained the last of her tea. "I should get back to the shop, but I'm glad we had a chance to talk, and I hope we'll become good friends."

"I'd like that." Brooke stood to share a parting hug with Erin. "And thanks for giving me some insight into Shaun."

"I promise, once you get to know him, you'll see what a great guy he is."

Brooke could only nod and hope Erin was right. Much as she respected and admired Shaun for his missionary service, and even though she did find his quirky sense of humor appealing, she had no intention of allowing his personal issues to sabotage the Christmas outreach.

Completing his final pass with the riding lawn mower, Shaun shut off the blades and steered the mower toward the garage. The combined smells of cut grass and gasoline filled his nostrils, but nothing stunk so bad as the way he'd handled things earlier with Brooke.

Years ago, his favorite seminary professor had cautioned him about his idealism. *"Not everything is black-and-white, Shaun. Demanding perfection from yourself or any other human being—at least in this life—will only bring disappointment."*

He was sure enough disappointed in himself, and he owed Brooke an apology. He wouldn't blame her if she'd already phoned Emily Ingram to plead for someone else to partner with for the Christmas service project. Maybe he should have simply gone along with one of the plans Brooke had presented. The three possibilities they'd initially agreed to consider weren't inherently bad, but after he'd had time to mull them over for a few days, he hadn't been able to reconcile how limited they were. He wanted to do more.

He *needed* to do more, or a month or a year or a decade from now, none of it would matter.

Shoulders sagging, he trudged out of the garage and gazed up through the live oak branches toward a cloudless autumn sky. "I get it, Lord. I'm pushing too hard again."

He'd back off, and he'd ask Brooke's forgiveness and hope she'd give him another chance. He tugged his phone from his back pocket and started to call her but then decided she deserved the courtesy of a face-to-face apology. Maybe he could snag a few minutes with her after church in the morning, after they'd both had more time to cool off.

As he started toward the house, a shiny red sedan slowed at the end of the driveway as if searching for an address. Then the car turned in, tires rumbling over the cattle guard. Kent was out with the herd, and Shaun didn't know enough about the area to offer directions, but he strode over anyway to help however he could.

With the tinted windows and the angle of the sun, he couldn't make out the driver's face—until the door opened and Brooke emerged. She slammed her door, then stood with feet apart and arms crossed. "Good, I found the right place. Hello again, Shaun."

"Uh, hi." His mouth tasted like dust and mown grass,

which didn't fully account for why he felt utterly speechless. "I—I was going to—"

She held up one hand. "Let me say what I came to say. As reluctant as I was at first, I've made a commitment to see this project through. I'd like us to try harder to work through our differences, but if you're calling it quits, I need to know now."

"I'm not." The words came out in a squeak. He cleared his throat and spoke more firmly. "I'm not quitting, Brooke."

Her brows shot up in surprise. "You're—you're not? I just figured—"

"I'm really sorry about leaving so abruptly after lunch." Finding his courage, he stepped close enough to see the golden glints in her brown eyes. He stuffed his hands in his pockets and shrugged. "When I get focused on something, I can be pretty opinionated, I know."

"That's putting it mildly," she muttered with a sidelong glance. Heaving a sigh, she went on, "You should also know I spoke with your sister this afternoon. She filled me in on a few things."

Wincing, Shaun lowered his head. "What exactly did Erin tell you?"

"About how you never do anything halfway. How you got really burned out on your last missionary posting." Brooke braced her hips against the fender. "How I should be patient and listen to your ideas."

Smiling inwardly, he sent his sister a mental thank-you. "So…you're willing to continue working with me?"

She didn't answer right away. "In my advertising career I dealt with more than my share of difficult clients, and if they didn't respect my professional expertise, I dropped them—politely, of course, but life is too short for that kind of stress."

"I get it. I'm a stress-inducing pain." Shaun studied his dirt-encrusted sneakers for a moment before peering up at her. "But you still haven't answered my question."

Hands lifted, Brooke gave an exaggerated huff. "Why else would I have driven all the way out here to clear the air when I could be shopping for things I don't need or pigging out on brownies and caramel lattes?"

He must have lost something in translation, but as long as she wasn't writing him off, he'd count his blessings. Which he probably hadn't been doing enough of lately, and which most likely had contributed to his lousy attitude. His lips twitched in a smile. "So I guess we should talk more about these outreach ideas."

"Yes, but not today." Lips tight, Brooke hiked her chin. "I'm not feeling particularly charitable at the moment."

"Toward me, or toward the world in general?"

"Mostly you."

Did she have any idea the effect her persistence was having on him, the way her eyes glinted with mischief even as she threw him a peevish pout? Shaun tamped down the niggling twinges of attraction. "Okay, then. You name the time and place."

"I'll check my calendar and call you tomorrow." She turned to open her car door.

"Maybe I'll see you at church?"

She mumbled something under her breath that sounded a lot like "Not if I see you first."

Watching her drive away, Shaun massaged the back of his neck. Crazy as it seemed, he was definitely experiencing more than friendly interest in Brooke Willoughby.

Pretty obvious the feeling wasn't mutual, but since he didn't foresee sticking around Juniper Bluff beyond the first of the year, he had no business dwelling on it. He just needed to stay on her good side long enough to organize the Christmas outreach.

In the meantime, he'd better pray even harder for direction about where he went from here, because half of the two weeks Henry Voss had given him had already zipped past, and Shaun didn't feel any closer to clarity than he had the day Henry had called.

Chapter Four

On their way out of the sanctuary following worship the next morning, Brooke's dad excused himself. "There's Lydia. I need to return her sunglasses."

Brooke's brows shot up. She grabbed her father's arm. "What are you doing with someone else's sunglasses?" A *strange woman's* sunglasses, more to the point.

"Because on the way home from Kerrville, I was sitting on the sunny side of the church van, so she was kind enough to lend me hers." He tried to shake off Brooke's hold.

She held on tighter. "But you have a perfectly good pair of sunglasses. I helped you pick them out while we were still living in LA, remember?"

"Forgot to tell you," Dad said with a grimace. "I accidentally left them at Mamacita's."

"Who on earth is Mamacita? And why were you at *her* place?"

Her father's eye roll insinuated the absurdity of Brooke's questions. "Mamacita's is the Mexican restaurant where the seniors group ate yesterday in Kerrville. Cute place. I should take you there sometime." He yanked his arm free. "Lydia's almost out the door. Gotta catch her."

Watching Dad hurry away, Brooke fought to keep from stamping her foot in a petulant show of annoyance.

Shaun ambled up beside her. "Everything okay?"

"Yes, everything's peachy." *Not.* Dad looked a little too cheery chatting it up with *Lydia*, and Brooke didn't know how she was supposed to feel about that.

"Okay, then." Shaun backed off a step. "Just wanted to ask if you'd thought more about scheduling another planning meeting."

"Right, we should do that soon." Giving herself a mental shake, she tore her gaze off her father and focused on Shaun. "Sorry, I'm a little worried about my dad."

"That's him in the corduroy blazer, right? Looks like he's made a new friend."

Exactly what worried her. Mom hadn't been gone a year yet. Dad had no business getting all smiley with other women. "This was a mistake," she muttered, barely aware she'd spoken aloud.

"Excuse me?" Shaun's tone hardened. "I thought we'd come to an understanding yesterday. If you feel that strongly about not wanting to work with me—"

"No, no, that isn't what I meant." She couldn't exactly blurt out all her misgivings about leaving a dream job in LA so she could bring her father back to Texas. Inhaling a calming breath, she briefly closed her eyes. When she opened them again, Dad was striding her way.

"Thanks for waiting, hon." He turned a curious expression upon Shaun. "Don't believe we've met. I'm Jim Willoughby, Brooke's dad."

"Pleasure, sir. Shaun O'Grady." He offered a handshake.

"Right, from the church committee." Gripping Shaun's hand, Dad leaned closer, his stage whisper a bit too obvious. "Guess you've already figured out this gal's all work and no play. I'd be mighty grateful if you could get her to loosen up a bit."

"Dad!" Heat rose in Brooke's face. She couldn't even look in Shaun's direction.

"Her work ethic is one of the things I already admire about her. But yeah," Shaun said, and she looked up in time to catch his wink, "I can see how she might occasionally take it to the extreme."

She looped her arm through her father's. "We should get going, Dad. Tripp and Diana will be waiting for us at the restaurant."

"Maybe your young fella would like to come along."

Young fella? Brooke could picture her face turning an even deeper shade of red. "I'm sure Shaun has other plans."

"Actually, I do," Shaun said, greatly relieving her mind. "My sister's expecting me at her house for lunch. But maybe another time."

Brooke smiled and nodded, while inside she was shouting, *No, no, no!* Nothing specifically against Shaun, but she preferred to direct her own social life, *without* her family's interference. "I'll call you later about scheduling a meeting."

"You've got my number."

As Shaun ambled away, Brooke's father shot her a disapproving frown. "Didn't have to be so abrupt with him, did you?"

"I wasn't abrupt." Well, maybe a little. She'd been in a perfectly good mood until the incident with Lydia and the sunglasses. Then any sense of equilibrium had flown out the window. "Anyway, Shaun is just my partner on this committee thing. I barely know the man."

"All the more reason to get better acquainted."

Best to ignore the remark. Arm still linked with her dad's, she started toward the exit.

Pastor Terry, greeting members at the door, beamed a smile as they approached. "Hope my suggestions for the Christmas outreach were helpful."

"Very. We're still narrowing down the possibilities."

"I'm sure whatever you and Shaun decide on will bless a lot of deserving families."

Deciding on a plan of action certainly seemed to be the sticking point. Brooke could only hope their future discussions were a lot more productive than yesterday's.

"This is not working." Brooke slapped shut the cover on her tablet computer and shoved back her chair. Seated at a corner table at Diana's Donuts Monday morning, she and Shaun had been at it for over an hour.

"You realize we're already into the first week of November." One arm braced on the table, Shaun leaned toward her. "Either we agree on *something* or we should stop right now and tell Emily to find somebody else."

"I'm not the one with the problem here," Brooke said, her voice rising. "Every single thing I suggest, you find a reason to shoot down. Either it isn't helping the right people, or it's too limited in scope, or—"

"I can't help it if nothing has felt right so far."

"Then maybe it's time to quit going on feelings and start looking at the facts. Beginning with number one, you are impossible—"

"Guys, guys!" Diana marched over and planted her

palms on the table between them. "I don't mind y'all meeting here, but you've got to keep it down."

"Sorry," they mumbled in unison.

Diana cast them each a warning glare before retreating to the counter.

Palm pressed to her forehead, Brooke strove for control. "Okay," she said, breathing out slowly, "can we back up and try this again?"

"Depends on what you mean. Keep trying to convince me your pragmatic action plans are the only intelligent approach—or try giving me a little credit for thinking outside the box so we can do some real good?"

"Shaun—"

He snorted. "Look, we both want the same thing here. At least, I think we do."

"Of course. The whole point is to help the people who need it most. And in the most efficient way possible."

"That's precisely where we diverge. Efficiency must never trump quality."

Brooke's cell phone vibrated near her left hand. Seeing her boss's name on the display, she couldn't help feeling grateful for the interruption. "Excuse me, I've got to take this."

Shaun's magnanimous sweep of his hand spoke volumes about his own need for a break. What had made her believe they could work through their differences and actually move forward with this project?

Stepping out to the sidewalk, she succumbed to a shiver and wished she'd taken the time to slip on her sweater. "Hi, Inez. Did you need something?"

"The Economic Development Committee meeting started fifteen minutes ago. You were supposed to be sitting in."

"Oh, no, I completely forgot." She swung around and shoved through the doughnut shop door. "I'm just across the square. I can be there in five."

"You haven't missed much yet. They're still chatting over coffee."

"I'll hurry." Disconnecting, Brooke grabbed her sweater and stuffed her tablet and phone into her tote. "We'll have to pick this up later, Shaun. I'm late for a meeting at the chamber."

He gathered up his jacket and steno pad and followed her out. "How long will you be?"

"I don't know." She barely slowed to reply. "This is my real job, and I can't afford to blow it."

"I understand. But we can't keep putting off a decision about the outreach, either." The smack of Shaun's sneakers kept pace beside her as she marched across First Street. "I can hang out in town for a while if you think you'll have time after your meeting."

"Fine. Suit yourself." Reaching the square, she broke into a jog, not easy in her slim-skirted power suit and heels. A few steps later, Shaun's panting breaths faded.

At the chamber office, she detoured to the ladies' room to run a brush through her breeze-tousled hair. After another painfully discouraging session with Shaun, she desperately needed to regain a semblance of composure before facing a roomful of Juniper Bluff's most successful business owners.

On her way to the conference room, Inez pulled her aside. "I know I told you this outreach project could benefit your long-term local business relationships, but not if it distracts you from your primary duties."

"It won't. We just got a little carried away with our discussion this morning." She took two steps, then spun around to face her boss. "No, it's more than that. Shaun O'Grady completely frustrates me. I'm not sure I can continue working with him."

Inez's right eyebrow lifted, and Brooke instantly wished she hadn't spoken. With a quick shake of her head, Inez gestured toward the conference room. "We'll take this up again after the meeting. Right now, you need to focus."

"Absolutely." Squaring her shoulders, Brooke mentally closed the door on Shaun O'Grady and strode into the meeting.

The buzz of conversation and laughter indicated the group was still in social mode. Inez stepped to the head of the table. "Has everyone met Brooke, our new communications manager?"

She recognized a few of the committee members, including Alan Glazer, her new insurance agent, and Wanda Flynn from WE Design. "I'm looking forward to getting to know all of you, and I'm here to help in any way I can."

Alan took charge of the meeting then, and Brooke settled in at the table with her tablet computer to take notes. As the group strategized on various ideas for promoting local businesses, she couldn't help noticing Alan's polite redirection whenever someone went off on a tangent or showed signs of defensiveness. His tact only underscored how poorly she and Shaun had been communicating. The main difference she could put her finger on was that all these people were experienced business owners and managers, whereas Shaun was every bit as idealistic as his sister had described.

Two different worlds, two different approaches. Was there no hope for compromise?

* * *

When are you going to learn to compromise? Shaun couldn't get around it—his own stubborn idealism had everything to do with the fact that he and Brooke couldn't come to consensus.

Well, maybe not *everything.* She needed to take some of the blame. Practicality, at least in certain circumstances, was highly overrated.

Killing time, Shaun meandered around the square. He glanced in shop windows without really seeing anything, all the while wondering why he didn't head back to the ranch and let Kent put him to work on some mindless chore. What made him think Brooke would be any more amenable to a rational discussion than she had been before rushing off to her meeting?

As long as he was browsing Main Street, he might as well stop in and say hi to his sister. A distant chime sounded as he stepped through the glass door of WE Design.

Erin's auburn head popped up from behind a display of decorative throw pillows. "May I help—oh, hi, Shaun. Didn't know you'd be in town today."

"Had another planning session with Brooke." He grimaced. "Didn't go so well."

"Shau-aun." She sounded like an exasperated schoolteacher.

"I know what you're going to say, so don't, okay?" Turning away, he fingered a leaf on a silk floral arrangement.

Erin stepped between him and the flowers. "I honestly thought being on this committee would be good for you, but I guess I was wrong. You're even grumpier now than you were when you first came home from Ethiopia."

"I'm not grumpy." Too bad his tone betrayed him.

"Mmm-hmm." Rolling her eyes, she repositioned the floral arrangement and then nudged him toward the table behind the counter. "Go sit down. I just heated water for tea."

"Tea is not going to fix me."

"No, but it'll keep *me* from wringing your neck."

While Erin prepared two mugs of Earl Grey, Shaun plopped into a chair and stretched out one leg. "Where's your partner this morning?"

"At a chamber of commerce meeting."

Probably the same one Brooke had to get to, and he didn't feel like being reminded about Brooke right now. He straightened as Erin set a mug in front of him and decided to change the subject. "Look at you, running an interior design business just like Mom. She'd have been so proud."

"Yeah, I'm kind of proud of myself," Erin mused as she sat across from him. "I'm just thankful Mom never had to know how terribly I messed up by marrying Payne."

"The creep's out of your life, and now you're engaged to a great guy. I couldn't be happier for you."

Erin raised her left hand to admire her antique sapphire engagement ring, a Ritter family heirloom. "If Greg hadn't talked me into moving to Juniper Bluff, I might never have met Kent." She glanced his way with a conspiratorial grin. "It could happen to you, too...if you'd let it."

"If by *it*, you mean finding true love, don't hold your breath. At least in my case, romance and missionary service have thus far proven incompatible."

Eyeing him over the rim of her mug, Erin quirked a grin. "Thus far, maybe, but not necessarily forever."

The door chime sounded and Wanda breezed in. "I'm

back, Erin. Oh, you've got company. Nice to see you again, Shaun."

"You, too, Wanda." Perfect timing, since he didn't seem able to avoid certain topics of conversation. He pushed up from the chair. "I should get going. I'm sure my sister has better things to do than shoot the breeze with me."

"What he means is," Erin stated as she gathered up their empty mugs, "he's tired of me telling him he needs to give romance a chance."

Laughing, Wanda dropped her purse onto a shelf behind the counter. "Anyone in particular you had in mind for your handsome and oh-so-available brother?"

"As a matter of fact—" Erin winked "—Shaun's been working with Brooke Willoughby on a Christmas outreach project. I think the real reason they can't come to terms is because Shaun's afraid he might actually be attracted to her."

Shaun snorted. "That's crazy."

"Is it?" Erin's narrowed gaze suggested she saw right through his quick denial.

"We don't see eye to eye on this project, that's all."

"Then maybe you ought to try adjusting your sights," Wanda said. "Because that gal is one sharp cookie. She had all kinds of workable ideas to kick off our Shop Juniper Bluff campaign—things we'd never have come up with on our own."

Now they were ganging up on him. Definitely time to leave. With a quick kiss to Erin's cheek and a nod to Wanda, he scuttled out the door.

Halting beneath the purple awning, he turned up his jacket collar against the crisp November breeze. He'd left his hatchback across the square in front of Diana's Donuts.

In twenty minutes he could be back at the ranch stacking hay bales or cleaning out feed buckets or whatever.

Or he could suck it up, walk down the block to the chamber of commerce and try—again—to work things out with Brooke.

A groan raked across his vocal chords. As loudly as his head was telling him to head for the ranch, his conscience screamed even louder that he needed to clear the air with Brooke. Besides, if he truly believed God was in control, then God must have had a good reason for pairing him up with her on this project.

Possibly to knock the ever practical and efficient Miss Willoughby down a peg and show her what serving in the Lord's name really looked like?

Holier-than-thou much? Shaun gave himself a mental lashing for such judgmental thoughts. For all he knew, Brooke had been placed in his life to teach him something about toning down his idealism.

Okay, he'd give it one more shot. And pray the Lord would soften his and Brooke's hearts for whatever lessons they each needed to learn.

Two minutes later, he stepped inside the lobby at the chamber of commerce. The casual, country-style decor in shades of green and tan made him feel like he'd just walked into a friend's living room. Glancing around, he spotted Brooke and a dark-haired gentleman deep in conversation in one of the corner seating arrangements.

She looked up, her eyes widening. "Shaun, I'm glad you're here."

That took him by surprise. "Didn't mean to interrupt, but we, uh, still have some unfinished business."

Her sheepish smile said she was equally uncomfortable with how they'd left things. "Come over and join us.

Have you met Alan Glazer? We've been talking about an interesting suggestion he had for the Christmas outreach."

Interest piqued, Shaun ambled over. After Brooke completed the introductions, he took the empty chair across from Alan.

"I handle the insurance needs for a small mobile home park a few miles west of town," Alan said. "Most of the residents are living at or below the poverty line, so the owner keeps rent as low as he can. Much as he'd like to implement improvements to make these families' lives easier, he's having enough trouble covering routine maintenance costs."

Brooke cast a hopeful look toward Shaun. "What do you think? Could this be our answer for doing the most good for the most families in a time frame the church committee could work with?"

He gnawed the inside of his lip while he pondered the possibilities. "We'd have a lot of options, that's for sure—tangible things we could do to benefit them well beyond the Christmas season."

After consulting his phone, Alan jotted something on the back of a business card. He handed it to Brooke. "Here's the contact information for the mobile home park. The owner is Carlos Zamora, and I know he'd appreciate anything you can do."

"We'll definitely look into this," Brooke said, then glanced at Shaun as if seeking his agreement.

He gave a firm nod. It was the closest they'd come to agreeing on anything since the night Emily Ingram drafted them for the project.

Chapter Five

After seeing Alan out, Brooke apologized to Shaun that with her full schedule the rest of the day, she couldn't spare more time to talk. "Anyway," she added with a guilty frown, "I have a feeling we've worn out our welcome at the doughnut shop."

"Probably so." Shaun released a half-hearted chuckle. "Know of any meeting rooms with soundproof walls?"

"We do tend to get a teensy bit vocal." She'd noticed Inez quietly closing her office door shortly after Shaun had arrived. "As for meeting here at the chamber...I'm afraid our reputation precedes us."

With a thoughtful glance toward the floor, Shaun rubbed his chin. "If we're seriously considering helping the trailer park families, we should make a trip out there to see firsthand what the needs are. Let me know when you're available, and I'll call Mr. Zamora about setting up a time."

Were they actually speaking like two civil adults? "Yes, let's arrange a visit as soon as possible. I've got to get to a lunch meeting, but I'll check my schedule as soon as I'm back at my desk."

Buoyed with renewed hope, Brooke told Shaun goodbye. As she started for her office, Inez stepped into the lobby.

"I didn't hear any yelling or screaming," her boss said. "Does that mean your Christmas project is back on track?"

"We're moving in the right direction...for now." She sighed. "If only I'd known about the mobile home park a week ago, maybe we could have avoided all the drama."

A mischievous smile creased Inez's lips. "Something tells me there's plenty more drama to come."

In a hurry to get to Casa Luis for the Juniper Bluff Lions Club meeting, she refused to waste time dwelling on her boss's observation. She rushed over to the restaurant, where she gave her full attention to mingling with more of the town's business and community leaders.

Returning afterward, she scanned her calendar for the next few openings in her schedule. After clearing the plan with Inez, she phoned Shaun. "I could get away for an hour or two starting around nine tomorrow. If that isn't convenient for Mr. Zamora, ask about late afternoon. I could possibly leave work a little early."

Shaun said he'd phone the mobile home park owner right away. Ten minutes later he called back. "We're on for nine thirty. He can't wait to meet us and show us around."

Brooke sucked in a breath. "Are we finally on the same page with this?"

"One step at a time...but yeah, we might be getting there." The relief in his tone matched hers. "I have directions to the park, but I wouldn't want you to mess up your clothes in my junker of a car. Would you mind picking me up?"

"No problem." She'd glimpsed his dented, faded-green Honda parked outside Diana's Donuts earlier. "I'll be there by nine fifteen."

Launching into several tasks she'd taken on for the Shop Juniper Bluff campaign, she lost track of the afternoon until Inez peeked in to remind her it was closing time. "See you at the Friends of the Library social in a couple of hours?"

Brooke feigned an enthusiastic smile. Who knew a small-town chamber of commerce could keep her hopping faster than a crazed jackrabbit? "I'll be there."

Arriving home for a quick bite of supper, she parked in the garage next to her dad's new compact-size silver pickup—the vehicle he'd claimed he *had* to have since they were living in Texas again. If it made him happy, great. She hurried inside. "I'm home, Dad," she called, "but I have to eat and run."

No reply.

She flung her tote and sweater on a chair and started pulling leftovers out of the fridge to warm up for supper. "Dad? Where are you?"

"Right here, hon." He ambled in from the living room. "Sorry, I was…"

The catch in his voice snapped her head up. Noticing his red-rimmed eyes, she dropped the plastic container of homemade chili on the counter and rushed over to wrap her arms around him. "Daddy, it's okay. Everything will be okay."

He nodded against her shoulder. "I know. Just got to thinking Thanksgiving's right around the corner and…"

"And you were missing Mom." Before her own emotions got the best of her, Brooke gave a loud sniff and directed her father toward the table. "Come sit down while I warm us up some supper. How does chili and a side salad sound?"

"Fine. But let me help." He was already grabbing lettuce and veggies from the crisper. "I'll make the salads."

"Thanks, Dad." Brooke could only smile. She'd definitely inherited her father's penchant for staying busy.

Mom, on the other hand, had been all about savoring each moment. How many times as children had Brooke and Tripp caught their mother just sitting and watching them as they played in the backyard? On birthdays and Christmases, she'd remind them to slow their frenetic pace of ripping open gifts so they could fully appreciate each one. And on Thanksgiving Day, one of Mom's favorite times of the year, no one dared sneak a bite of turkey or cranberry sauce until each person at the table had shared a word of gratitude.

This year, though, Brooke had been trying hard to not even think about the holiday, the one-year anniversary of her mother's death. Maybe the chance to skip right past Thanksgiving explained her willingness to devote so much energy to the Christmas outreach. Christmas would be hard in its own way, but nothing like reliving the most painful day of her life.

Sitting down to supper a little while later, they ate in silence for a few minutes. Then Dad speared a cherry tomato with his fork and stared at it. "Diana said she and her parents would host this year."

Her thoughts rushing ahead to tonight's library function, Brooke took a moment to catch his meaning. When she did, she almost couldn't swallow her mouthful of chili. "Actually, I was thinking about booking a vacation rental at the coast. We could spend a couple of days in Galveston or Corpus Christi, have some great seafood..."

Dad's frown clearly communicated his disapproval.

"I meant all of us," she continued, defensiveness

creeping into her tone. "As hard as Tripp and Diana both work, I'm sure they could use a weekend getaway. Diana's parents would be welcome to come along, too."

"With livestock to tend to, it's probably not that easy for the Matthewses to pack up and leave." Dad finished chewing a bite of salad. "Besides, it's not fair to expect everybody else to change their plans because you don't want to be around for the holiday."

"And you do?" Irritation rising, Brooke laid aside her spoon. "Dad—"

He held up one hand. "I know it'll be hard, honey, but you can't outrun the memories." His voice shook with vehemence as he added, "And I can't understand why you'd want to, because I sure don't. Your mom was everything to me."

The image of her father looking so chummy with the woman at church yesterday flashed in her brain. "Obviously not *everything*, since you've been so quick to move on with *Lydia*."

Dad's mouth fell open. "Brooke Elaine Willoughby. Don't you dare presume to judge my feelings."

Swamped with remorse, she shoved away from the table. "I'm sorry. I just—I need to get ready for the library thing. Forget what I said, okay?"

Shaun could tell the moment he climbed into Brooke's car Tuesday morning that she wasn't her usual confident self. "Not having second thoughts about helping the trailer park families, I hope?"

"What? No." A shaky laugh erupted as she moved the gearshift to Reverse. "I attended a Friends of the Library event last night, and after all the schmoozing, I had a hard time getting to sleep."

"Schmoozing. Done plenty of that with my mission-ary support raising." Although something told him there was more going on with her than social fatigue, because that alone didn't account for the grim set of her mouth or the way her knuckles whitened around the steering wheel.

With jerky motions, she backed around and aimed the car toward the road. "Okay, where are we headed?"

"Take this road back the way you came, then turn left at the four-way stop."

When they reached the intersection, Brooke's mood seemed to lighten. "This will take us past Serenity Hills Guest Ranch. My dad and I stayed there a couple of times when we visited Tripp before he and Diana got married."

"That's where my brother heads up the camping pro-gram for disadvantaged kids."

"Greg—yes. I remember meeting him out there last year." Brooke turned thoughtful again. "I know you see your sister often. How about Greg? Are you close with him?"

Glancing out the window, Shaun shrugged. "As close as brothers can be who've spent most of the last fifteen years living thousands of miles apart."

"That's kind of how it was with our family until Dad and I moved here. At least I had my parents with me in LA…until Mom died." Growing quiet again, Brooke kept her eyes on the road.

Pastoral instincts had Shaun wondering if he should encourage her to talk more. On the other hand, it might be easier to work together if they didn't delve too deeply into each other's personal lives. He unfolded the slip of paper where he'd jotted down the directions. "After we pass Serenity Hills, the trailer park is another two miles or so. The entrance will be on the left."

Brooke glanced his way. "Seriously? You haven't been using the GPS on your phone?"

"No need. Mr. Zamora's directions were pretty straightforward."

"*Or so* is kind of vague, don't you think? I prefer it when the app voice tells me exactly where to turn."

Relieved to see Brooke's feisty side returning, Shaun snickered. "Where's your sense of adventure? The worst that could happen is we go flying by the turnoff and have to circle back. You *do* know how to make a U-turn?"

She glared. "Okay, there's Serenity Hills. I'm checking my odometer right now. When it counts up two miles, I'm slowing way down. Will there be a sign or something?"

"Whitetail Valley Mobile Home Park." Scanning ahead, Shaun leaned forward in his seat. "That could be it just past those cedar trees."

"I see it." Brooke braked slightly and hit her left-turn signal. "Wow, if the park is in as much disrepair as their sign, we'll have our work cut out for us."

Shaun had to agree. The large wooden sign sat askew, barely clinging to the two wooden posts it was nailed to. Peeling paint had left the deer with one antler, and the white tail was missing altogether. With almost half the letters in the sign unreadable, it looked like "Whit Val Mob me ark."

Making the turn, Brooke followed a potholed asphalt lane for thirty yards or so, then pulled into an equally decrepit parking area. A sign over the door of a square cinder block building indicated this was the office.

A middle-aged Latino man stepped outside and waved.

Wearing faded jeans and a quilted vest over a flannel shirt, he smiled broadly as Shaun and Brooke climbed from the car. "Welcome, my friends. I see you found us okay."

"Your directions were perfect." Shaun angled a grin toward Brooke. After introductions, they followed Mr. Zamora inside to a small sitting area.

Brooke looked askance at the lumpy sofa and chairs beneath mismatched ragged throws. Shaun had experienced much more rustic conditions on the mission field, but he could understand Brooke's hesitation. He should have suggested she forget the dress-for-success pantsuit and heels, and change for the office after they got back to town.

"Would you care for coffee?" Mr. Zamora started toward the counter behind his cluttered desk.

"Love some." Shaun settled onto the sofa.

Lowering herself onto the opposite end, Brooke gingerly patted the cushion next to her, then seemed to breathe a sigh of relief. Apparently, she'd satisfied herself that the furnishings were clean if not new. "Yes. Coffee. Thanks."

Mr. Zamora returned with three steaming mugs, then took the chair at Shaun's left. "Your call yesterday had me greatly intrigued. If there is anything your church group can do to make things better for my tenants, we would all be most grateful."

Shaun took a careful sip of his coffee. "Maybe you could start by telling us about any specific needs you have."

"Where to begin?" Regret and resignation shadowed the man's expression. "Everyone here is struggling to provide for themselves and their families, just as I am. My wife and I are both Mexican immigrants. She works in town at the supermarket, and besides managing the park, I also work four nights a week as a custodian at the assisted living center."

Fingers wrapped around her mug, Brooke sat forward. "No wonder it's so hard to keep up. How many tenants do you have?"

"We have spaces for twenty mobile homes. Seventeen of those are occupied." Mr. Zamora glanced over his shoulder toward the window. "Our resident families are quite diverse—Latinos, Asians, refugees from Africa and Syria—"

Shaun felt a prick beneath his breastbone. "You have a Syrian family?"

"Yes, an older couple. For a time, they were receiving resettlement assistance from a church in Kerrville. The husband has a heart condition and is unable to work."

"What about children?" Brooke asked. "Are there any young families?"

Mr. Zamora brightened. "Oh, yes. When the school bus pulls up this afternoon, the park will be noisy with children's laughter. I only wish…" He grimaced. "Perhaps we should take a walk. I can show you the sad condition of our playground, among other things. Then you can decide for yourselves what you might be able to do for us."

A sense of urgency churning in his gut, Shaun gulped the rest of his coffee. While Brooke finished hers, he went to the window and gazed down the long row of mobile homes. Some sat amid tiny patches of sparse grass, while other lawn areas had been spread with gravel. A weed here and there poked through, but otherwise, the park appeared tidy. A few tenants had brightened their surroundings with small flowerbeds or potted plants. Even so, the overall impression was a bleak attempt at subsistence.

Coming up beside him, Mr. Zamora said, "You seemed to have a special interest in the Syrian couple."

"Several years ago, I spent some time in Jordan helping Syrian refugees."

"You are a missionary?" The man sighed. "I sometimes think of my work here in that way. Many people showed kindness to my wife and me when we first came here from Mexico. But that was many years ago. Things are much different now, and if I can provide a safe haven for others striving for a better life, that is my mission."

"Excuse me," Brooke said, joining them at the window. "I hesitate to ask this, but…is anyone here illegally?"

"No, I assure you, every one of my tenants is a US citizen. I could not risk having this facility shut down because of immigration issues."

"Good to know," Shaun said. His respect for Carlos Zamora deepened. "Ready to show us around?"

Flats—better yet, sneakers—would have been a much wiser choice of footwear. Brooke had to walk on tiptoe to keep from snagging her three-inch heels in the pitted asphalt lane.

Mr. Zamora motioned toward a long, flat-roofed structure behind the main office. "This building serves as a meeting and recreation room and also houses our laundry facilities." He sighed. "Unfortunately, two of our washing machines are currently out of service until funds are available for repair."

"Can we see inside?" Shaun was already bustling up the cracked sidewalk to the entrance.

Hurrying to keep up, Brooke wished paranoia hadn't prompted her to leave her tablet computer locked in the car. She should be compiling a list of possibilities for helping these families.

Beyond the rec building, she glimpsed a corner of the playground. A dark-haired woman, obviously several months pregnant, chased after a toddler heading for a lopsided slide.

"Marisol, be careful or you'll hurt yourself." The woman scooped up the child moments before she would have darted up the bent ladder rungs.

Brooke caught her breath. No reason to worry about taking notes, because the needs before her would be etched in her memory for a long, long time.

"Coming, Brooke?" Shaun's tight expression said he'd already taken a quick look inside the building.

"This is all so sad," she murmured as she stepped past him.

"This is nothing. I've seen a whole lot worse."

Her gaze swept the drab walls and faded vinyl flooring. Apparently, *recreation* amounted to a lopsided ping-pong table and a bookshelf stacked with tattered paperbacks and a few ancient board games.

Across the room, two older couples seated around a card table looked up with curious smiles. Mr. Zamora motioned Brooke and Shaun over. "Let me introduce you to George and Mariam Paulos, and their neighbors Luke and Esther Tran."

The men stood to shake hands with Shaun as their wives hurried over to greet Brooke with warm smiles and air kisses. The Trans appeared to be Asian, while the olive-complected Pauloses had a distinctive Mediterranean look. When Shaun greeted them with *"Marhaban, kayfa haaluka,"* she realized they must be the Syrian couple.

The Pauloses shared smiles of recognition as Mr. Paulos pumped Shaun's hand even harder. "*Jayyid jiddan. Ahlan wa sahlan*! You speak Arabic?"

"Badly," Shaun said with a self-deprecating chuckle. "It's been a few years since I've had a chance to practice."

Brooke tapped Shaun's arm. "What did y'all just say to each other?"

"I said, 'Hello, how are you?' And Mr. Paulos said, 'Very well. Welcome.'"

"Please, call me George," the man said. "It's a pleasure to meet you both."

"You, too." Feeling entirely out of her element, Brooke laced her fingers. "Looks like you have a bridge game going. Don't let us keep you."

"Yes, we should continue." Mr. Zamora excused himself to the couples before showing Shaun and Brooke through a door at the back of the room.

The pungent smells of detergent and bleach assaulted Brooke's nose. On one side of the room, the only working washer vibrated through its spin cycle. A waist-high table stacked with folded laundry filled the center space, and on the other side, two dryers rumbled.

"Only a few of our tenants have washers and dryers in their homes," the manager explained. "In the evenings and on weekends, there are usually several families waiting to use the machines."

Brooke stepped closer to one of the washers, then turned to Mr. Zamora with a questioning look. "I thought these would be coin-operated. The residents use them for free?"

"They furnish their own supplies, of course." The man shrugged. "They have struggles enough without worrying about finding enough quarters to do their laundry."

Brooke had no words. She'd never known a single

day of want, at least not like this. Yes, she'd been inconvenienced by delayed flights or the occasional car breakdown, even had her own washer go on the fritz a few years ago. But a repairman had come right out and gotten it up and running in a matter of hours.

Shaun had devoted his life to serving people in far less favorable conditions than these. How did he do it? What kind of person did it take to forgo the creature comforts middle-class America took for granted, to move thousands of miles from home and family, to immerse oneself in a foreign culture and take on the problems of those people as your own?

"Brooke, are you okay?" Shaun stood in front of her, worry creasing his brow.

She sniffed, only then noticing the trickle of wetness sliding down her cheek. Flicking it away, she replied softly, "I'm suddenly realizing what a privileged life I've led."

He gave a solemn nod. "Hard to get your head around the fact that as much as eighty percent of the world's population survives on less than ten dollars a day."

Ten dollars a day, scarcely three hundred dollars a month... She slowly shook her head. "How..."

With a quick squeeze of her hand, Shaun turned to Mr. Zamora. "Brooke needs to get back to work soon, but you've given us plenty to think about. Can we get back with you after we've had a chance to discuss some options?"

"By all means." The man wore a look of concern as he walked them to Brooke's car. "Please know that we would be most grateful for whatever small assistance your committee might be able to offer."

Climbing behind the wheel, Brooke sat in silence for several moments. With a final glance down the dreary line of mobile homes, she turned the car toward the road.

She was glad Shaun didn't make an attempt at conversation, because she needed more time to process her thoughts and emotions.

A mile or so beyond Serenity Hills Guest Ranch, she glimpsed the new housing development they'd passed on the drive out. Elegant brick homes in various stages of construction surrounded a massive horse barn and covered arena. The sign at the road proclaimed Luxury Ranchettes Starting at $899K.

What a contrast with what she'd just observed, and the Whitetail Valley Mobile Home Park residents had to pass this development every time they drove into Juniper Bluff.

"Ready to talk yet?" Shaun asked a few minutes later.

"Not quite." Approaching the road leading to Kent's ranch, she slowed and flipped her turn signal.

"We can't put this off too long. Not if we're going to accomplish anything by Christmas."

"I know." She cast him a tight-lipped smile as she made the turn. "But I've got a million things going on with chamber business this afternoon. And tonight I need to sit down with no distractions and think about everything."

"Good idea. We both need to approach this with clearer heads."

"And a lot less arguing," she said with a pointed stare.

Shaun ducked his head. "Agreed."

Chapter Six

Two days went by without hearing from Brooke, and Shaun was getting antsy. They were well into the first full week of November. If they didn't hammer out the specifics ASAP, they'd have to settle for delivering Christmas turkeys and assorted canned goods. So much for providing the Whitetail Valley families with any kind of meaningful assistance.

Time was also running out for Shaun to answer his missions director about the call to serve in Jordan again. Why did he have such mixed feelings about returning to the mission field, especially to a country he loved? Was this indecision the Holy Spirit trying to tell him something? Or was he deliberately avoiding God's will?

On Thursday evening as he and Kent washed up the supper dishes, his cell phone rang. The screen displayed Brooke's name and number—finally. He answered on his way to the living room.

"Sorry I didn't get back to you sooner," she began. "Things have been pretty hectic at the office."

Shaun bypassed Kent's lazy yellow Lab mix curled

up on the recliner and plopped onto one end of the sofa. "I began to worry you were purposely avoiding me."

"Of course not. And I haven't been *completely* preoccupied with work. I've also done a lot of thinking about the families at the trailer park."

"Me, too. When do you want to get together and talk through some ideas?"

"The sooner, the better. I just got off the phone with Emily Ingram, and she's calling a committee meeting Monday night so we can get the ball rolling."

About time, Shaun didn't say.

"I have an early lunch meeting tomorrow, but since it's Friday, Inez said I could take the rest of the day off to work on the Christmas outreach. Are you free in the afternoon?"

"Sure. Want to come out here to Kent's place?" He chuckled. "That way, we don't have to worry about disturbing anyone if our discussion gets a bit too, uh, *intense*."

"What—us? Argue?" she scoffed. It was nice to hear a touch of lightness in her tone. "How does two o'clock sound?"

"I'll be watching for you. And remember, this is a working ranch. You might want to change into something more casual than your dress-for-success duds."

"No spiked heels, I promise. See you tomorrow."

Kent sauntered in as Shaun laid aside his phone. "Gathered that was Brooke. How's it going with the Christmas project?"

"There's hope on the horizon." Shaun had told Kent about their visit to the mobile home park. "She's coming out tomorrow so we can hammer out a plan."

"I'll believe it when I see it." Grinning, Kent gave his

old dog a scratch behind the ears, then sprawled on the other end of the sofa. "Changing the subject, Erin and I were talking wedding plans again today, and…"

Shaun's stomach tensed. "If this is about officiating—"

"You know how happy it would make Erin. What's holding you back?"

He'd be forever grateful for their patience, but how could he explain what he didn't fully understand himself? He sat forward and massaged his temples. "Ever since I returned to the States, I've been trying to get back in touch with why I chose missionary service in the first place. Trying to get back in touch with God, to be completely honest."

Kent nodded slowly. "After Afghanistan, I kept my distance from God for a long time. Erin gets all the credit for showing me the way back." He gave Shaun a good-natured poke in the arm. "Maybe Brooke can do the same for you."

"Not so sure about that." He pondered what little he'd discerned about Brooke's faith life. "Yeah, she goes to church and all, but I get the feeling she's got her own issues with the Lord."

"One thing I've learned the last few months is that faith is a journey, and it isn't always a smooth ride. If you fall off the horse, you've got two options. Either start walking and hope you get where you're going on your own, or climb back on and hold on for dear life."

Shaun cast his future brother-in-law a wry grin. "That your version of cowboy theology?"

"Does it work for you?"

"Not a bad metaphor, actually."

Ankles crossed, Kent stretched out his legs. "So how

about climbing back on that horse and saying you'll do our wedding ceremony?"

A weak laugh erupted from Shaun's throat. Both touched and humbled by Kent's insistence, he gave his head a helpless shake. "Can I just say I'll think about it?"

"Nope, but you can say you'll *pray* about it." Kent stuck out his hand. "Deal?"

"Deal."

The next morning, Shaun awoke with a sore shoulder, likely the result of one of two things—hefting those fifty-pound sacks of grain he'd moved from Kent's pickup to the feed room yesterday, or the arm-twisting Kent had given him about officiating at the wedding.

Probably a little of both.

With early-morning chores done and Kent at his part-time job at the hardware store, Shaun started a fresh pot of coffee. While it perked, he went upstairs to fetch his Bible and journal. For years, he'd made a habit of studying the Scriptures first thing every morning and journaling his thoughts and prayers. Now, more than ever, he needed to double down on the prayer front.

After pouring a mug of coffee, he spread his materials in front of him on the kitchen table. Opening to his last entry in the journal, dated nearly two weeks ago, he cringed. He hadn't written a single word since the day Henry Voss had called about the church position in Jordan. No wonder God was having a hard time getting through to him.

Recalling a passage that had often reassured him, he turned to Psalm 32: *I will instruct thee and teach thee in the way which thou shalt go: I will guide thee with mine eye.*

The path forward might be obscured to Shaun's vision, but God saw everything clearly. The only thing God expected of him was to faithfully take the next step. Standing still and doing nothing was not an option.

Blowing out a sharp breath, he mentally replayed Henry's call. He still missed the team he'd worked with in Jordan, one of the most fulfilling assignments of his missionary career. The opportunity to return had to be a sign from God…didn't it? Henry had asked for an answer by tomorrow. All Shaun had to do was call him back and say yes.

He reached for his phone and scrolled through his contacts for Henry's number. His thumb hovered over the call icon.

With a shudder, he laid the phone face down on the table, then palmed his eye sockets. Serving the Lord was all he'd ever wanted. His reservations made no sense.

He snatched up the phone, and this time he didn't hesitate. "Henry, glad I caught you. About that assignment in Jordan…"

"I take it you've made a decision?"

"I—" His glance fell again to the psalm he'd just read. *I will instruct thee… I will guide thee…* His fist clenched. He squeezed his eyes closed. "I need more time. This is turning out to be a tougher decision than I expected."

The silence on the other end of the line was deafening. Finally, Henry spoke. "As I told you the last time we talked, I believe this position is ideal for you, a perfect match for your skills and experience. What's holding you back, Shaun? Is there anything you haven't shared with me?"

"I don't know what's going on, Henry. I'm just not

sensing God's direction about this, and I don't want to jump ahead of His will."

"That's wise," Henry said with a sigh. "But not the answer I was hoping for. I can hold off a little longer, I suppose. A couple more weeks is all I can give you. Perhaps the Lord's guidance will be clearer by then."

Shaun could only hope. They said their goodbyes, and with his coffee now cold, he reheated it in the microwave before trying once again to delve into prayer and God's Word.

Dress casual, huh? Brooke knew how. She really did. She had an impressive selection of designer jeans to choose from—three shades of denim blue, plus black, gray, violet and mustard yellow. She didn't wear the yellow ones much, but an overly exuberant store associate had assured her it was the latest color trend and she simply must have them to go with the purple tunic sweater she'd fallen in love with.

That pairing didn't seem appropriate for an afternoon at a cattle ranch, though, so she opted for her faded blue skinny jeans with an oversize pink plaid flannel shirt worn over a white turtleneck. Tall brown boots and a fleece-collared distressed bomber jacket completed the outfit.

On her way through the kitchen, she found her dad finishing up a phone call. "Who was that?"

"Just a friend from church." An uneasy smile fluttered across his lips. He turned away to put something in the dishwasher.

Lydia of the infamous lost sunglasses incident, perhaps? Brooke decided she'd rather not know. She scooped up her tote and car keys. "I'll be working on the Christmas project with Shaun all afternoon. Call if you need anything."

"Have a good meeting, honey. By the way, we're invited to Tripp and Diana's for supper. Seven o'clock."

"I should be home in plenty of time." Provided she and Shaun didn't take too long coming to terms.

On the drive out to Kent Ritter's place, she mentally reviewed her observations from their tour of the mobile home park. With so many practical needs, it shouldn't be hard to come up with a plan of action they could present to the outreach committee on Monday evening. Once the others got involved, hopefully she could focus more on her real job and not have to think so much about the approaching holidays.

As she pulled up behind Shaun's ancient green hatchback, a tail-wagging yellow dog with its tongue hanging out trotted over to her car. The galumphing critter looked friendly enough, so she eased the door open. "Back up, doggy. These are clean jeans and I'd rather not have your slobber on them."

"Skip, here, boy!" Shaun hurried over to grab the dog's collar. "Sorry, he doesn't know a stranger."

"It's okay. I'm an animal lover, but smaller pets are more my style. Like a miniature poodle or schnauzer. Maybe a nice little short-haired kitty that doesn't shed much." Stepping from the car, she gave the Lab a tentative pat on the head. "Nothing personal, fella."

Shaun snickered. "I don't think Skip is easily offended. But I should warn you, he pretty much has the run of Kent's house."

Grateful she'd heeded Shaun's suggestion about appropriate attire, she dusted a couple of stray dog hairs off her hand and adjusted the strap of her tote. "Shall we get to work?"

With the dog ambling alongside, Shaun showed her through the screened back porch and into a cheery yellow kitchen. "Thought we could work here at the table."

She pulled out a chair and set down her tote, then did a slow turn. "Hard to believe a bachelor lives here. I'm guessing your sister had a lot to do with the decorating?"

"It's partly what brought them together. Kent's house is a Juniper Bluff historical site, and Erin helped him spruce it up for the sesquicentennial celebration the town's planning for next spring."

"Yes, I've heard. A couple of our chamber committees are already discussing their part."

Shaun offered a brief smile as he pulled out a chair. "I'll have to get Erin and Kent to send me pictures."

"I guess you'll be on to something else by then." The unexpected pang of disappointment hollowed out Brooke's stomach. Straining for a smile of her own, she took a seat catercorner from Shaun and opened her tablet computer.

They began by comparing notes about the various needs at the park, then compiled them into a comprehensive list. At least there was no reason to argue about the state of the playground or laundry facilities. And the rec room could certainly be improved upon, beginning with fresh paint and new furniture, games and books.

"A wide-screen TV and DVD player would be a nice addition, too," Brooke suggested. "Maybe we could get one of the stores in town to donate some family-friendly movies."

Shaun shook his head. "Let's not get ahead of ourselves. Practically speaking, repairing or replacing the washers and dryers makes the most sense."

"Wait a minute...wait a minute." Narrowing one eye, Brooke tapped her temple with her index finger. "Aren't you the same guy who only a few days ago went all ballistic about my *pragmatic* suggestions?"

"I never meant to imply being pragmatic was always a bad thing. And anyway, you weren't exactly complimentary about my *thinking outside the box.*"

Brooke sat back and locked her arms across her chest. "So what *are* we going for here? Pragmatic or progressive? No-nonsense or no-holds-barred?"

"Now you're being ridiculous." Jaw clenched, Shaun slammed his steno pad shut and shoved away from the table. "I should have known we couldn't get through one hour without devolving into an argument."

"That's only because you are the stubbornest, most short-sighted—"

The back door flew open and a guy in a cowboy hat barged in. "Hey, you two! Dial it back a notch, will you?" Whipping off his hat, he gave a disgusted eye roll. "It's no wonder Diana threw you out of the doughnut shop."

"Sorry, Kent." Shaun stood, hands on hips. "Guess we got a little carried away."

"Again," Brooke murmured. "Hello, I'm Brooke Willoughby. We met briefly at the outreach meeting at church." She rose and offered her hand, then thought better of it when she noticed the grime clinging to Kent's clothes.

"Right, Tripp's sister." As if reading her mind, Kent scraped his palms up and down his jeans before shaking hands, and then managed to do so with only the tips of his fingers. Mouth in a twist, he cast thoughtful glances between Shaun and Brooke. "Seeing as how y'all don't seem to be getting anywhere, how about taking a breather? Nothin' better for clearing the head than a little fresh country air."

Shaun shared a sheepish half smile with Brooke. "Maybe a short break would do us both some good. Want to stretch your legs?"

"Actually," Kent began, "I was about to suggest a horseback ride."

Brooke's heartbeat quickened with the thrill of a fond memory. "My grandparents used to have horses, but it's been years since I've ridden."

"Then let's go." Kent motioned toward the door. "You're game, aren't you, Shaun?"

"Uh, I guess so." He didn't look quite so certain. "But we can't take too long. We still have a lot to discuss."

"Nothin' says you can't talk and ride at the same time." Kent detoured to the fridge. "I'll even pack some snacks for the trail."

Minutes later, he'd filled an insulated saddlebag with drinks, cheese slices, a couple of apples and a package of crackers. Grabbing jackets, Brooke and Shaun followed him out to the barn, where a big black horse was already saddled and waiting in a stall.

Brooke reached across the stall gate to stroke the mare's muzzle. "Who's this?"

"That's Jasmine, my trusty cow horse." Kent opened the next stall and led a sorrel mare into the aisle. "This is Posey. I'll help you get her tacked up. Shaun, you can saddle Petunia."

Brooke turned to Shaun with a mischievous grin. "Oh, so you do ride."

"Only under duress." He led the other mare into the

aisle and clipped cross ties to either side of her halter. "It was pretty much a prerequisite for living here with Kent."

Forgetting any concerns about keeping her clothes spotless, Brooke took over with the curry and hoof pick while Kent brought a saddle and bridle from the tack room. As she fastened the cinch and adjusted stirrup lengths, excitement pulsed through her as if she were ten years old again. After Kent fitted her with a riding helmet, he boosted her into the saddle. She took up the reins and waited with barely concealed impatience while Shaun finished tacking his horse and everyone was mounted.

Riding Jasmine, Kent led the way out of the barn. Though the November breeze carried a chill, the sky was crystal clear and the sun warm. Touches of fall color brightened the landscape, and the air smelled of mountain cedar mixed with hints of horse hide and cow patties.

"How ya doin' back there?" Kent called from up front.

"Fine, just fine." Brooke didn't think she'd stopped grinning since Kent had first suggested the ride. She glanced over her shoulder at Shaun, who appeared to be concentrating entirely too hard. "Hey, this isn't brain surgery. We're supposed to be relaxing and having fun."

"Fun. Right." He faked a smile.

Drawing up on the reins slightly, she came even with Shaun's horse. "Sorry we argued again."

"Me, too." He blew out a tense breath, then smiled for real. Just a small one, enough to let her know he was sincere. He was a pastor, after all. About time he used his ministerial training to try to find some common ground. "What's the deal with us, anyway?"

She harrumphed. "When you figure it out, let me know."

They rode in pleasant silence across the rocky terrain. Small clumps of cattle grazed on either side, and somewhere in the distance a creek burbled. A little farther along, Kent pointed to a spreading live oak. "Here's my favorite spot for a picnic. Y'all can dismount and take the picnic stuff over while I tend to the horses."

Shaun eased out of the saddle, then handed his horse's reins to Kent. Before he could come over to help Brooke down, she swung her leg over and dropped to the ground. Shaun whistled his appreciation. "You make it look too easy."

"Just like riding a bike." She walked her horse over to Kent, who took the reins and then handed down a rolled quilt and the insulated saddlebag.

With the quilt spread beneath the tree, Brooke knelt to help Shaun set out the food. Noticing it had grown quiet, she glanced around. "Where'd Kent take the horses?"

Shaun sat back on his heels, his gaze sweeping left and right. "Good question."

"He wouldn't just leave us here, would he?"

"No way." Shaun's nervous laugh didn't reassure her. He stood. "Kent? Hey, Kent!"

No reply.

Now Brooke was getting nervous. She had no idea how far they'd ridden, much less how to find their way back. "If this is his idea of a joke, it's not funny."

"Something tells me he didn't intend it as a joke." Heaving a groan, Shaun lowered himself onto the quilt. "More likely, he's trying to make a point."

"Point?" Clambering to her feet, she peered through the trees. "Well, I don't have time for this kind of thing.

Go after him. Make him bring those horses back right now."

With a grim shake of his head, Shaun shifted to lean against the tree trunk. "Won't do any good. I'm sure he's halfway back to the house by now." He passed her a canned drink. "He'll be back for us eventually. Might as well chill for a while and enjoy the snacks and fresh air."

Seething, Brooke stared at Shaun, then at the frosty cola she held. She *was* getting hungry, come to think of it. And since it didn't look like she had much choice…

Chapter Seven

When Brooke dropped to her knees and popped the top on her drink, Shaun released an inner sigh of relief. He'd learned pretty quickly that though his future brother-in-law was a man of few words, he had other ways of getting his message across.

Hard to misread Kent's intent this afternoon: *whatever's going on between you two, quit being so bullheaded and work it out.*

To himself, he muttered, "I'm beginning to believe that's been God's purpose for us all along."

Brooke narrowed her gaze. "What did you say?"

"Sorry, thinking out loud." He pulled the saddlebag closer and brought out the fruit, crackers and cheese. "Here, help yourself."

Sitting cross-legged, Brooke took a napkin from the saddlebag and polished an apple, then crunched into it. "You said something about God's purpose. Tell me what you meant."

"Don't take this wrong," he began with an uneasy glance, "but I'm wondering if the reason you and I got thrown together was so we could sand down each other's rough edges."

She studied him while chewing another bite of apple. "Your rough edges are pretty obvious. But as for *moi*..." A teasing grin turned up the corners of her mouth.

"Ah, yes, please forgive me. There's *nothing* the least bit prickly about totally together Brooke Willoughby." He helped himself to some crackers and cheese, then had to duck when Brooke tossed her apple at him. "Hey, now!"

"You deserved that." She held out her hand. "Here, give it to me and I'll save it for my horse. That is, if Kent really does come back for us."

As she reclaimed the apple, their fingertips grazed. Shaun's breath caught, and he found himself irrationally curious about what it would be like to kiss her. Shaking off the thought, he reached for his soft drink and took a nervous gulp. "I told you, he'll be back."

Brooke shifted to take in the scenery. "At least it's a nice day. I'm too used to California weather."

"So you liked it out there?"

"A lot. I loved my job and my cute little house in the 'burbs. Oh, and the shopping was great—anything I ever needed or wanted." She hugged her knees and sighed. "LA is an exciting place to live."

"Even with all the traffic congestion?"

"There is that one teensy inconvenience." Glancing over her shoulder, she smiled. "But those long commutes gave me lots of time to listen to some excellent audio-books."

Why did it sound as if she were trying to convince herself? Maybe the overly chirpy lilt to her voice? "If you loved it so much, why come to Juniper Bluff?"

Her eyes closed briefly. "For my dad. I knew he'd never be happy again until I brought him home to Texas."

"You mentioned your mother passed away. They were living with you in California?"

"Only for the last few years." She took a sip of her drink, then set the can aside. "My mom had kidney disease, but with her particular blood type, finding a donor match was next to impossible. I didn't want Dad trying to care for her by himself, so I brought them to live with me." Her chin trembled. "She died last year on Thanksgiving Day."

He couldn't resist reaching out for her hand. "I'm sorry."

"Thank you." She sniffed back a tear. "It isn't helping that my dad and Tripp and Diana are all gung-ho about planning Thanksgiving dinner, when all I want to do is run away to a white, sandy beach somewhere."

"They're probably just trying to make some good memories to help get past the sad ones."

"Maybe so, but I'm not ready." Her fingers felt soft and fragile as he cradled them in his palm. Her eyes met his, and she offered a brief but grateful smile. "So enough about me," she said with a forced laugh. "You're the mystery man about town. Everyone keeps asking me what your story is. For some odd reason, they think I must have the inside track."

"That's crazy." He should let go of her hand now, but he didn't want to. The pad of his thumb slipped across one of her glossy pink nails.

After a couple of electricity-charged moments, she eased her hand free. "Um, you're supposed to say something now."

He straightened and cleared his throat. "I've pretty

much told you everything worth knowing. I'm just a burned-out missionary pastor waiting for the Lord to show me what comes next."

Brooke harrumphed. "That's a cop-out answer if I ever heard one."

"Which part—the fact that I'm burned out, or that I'm waiting for God's direction?"

"Neither." She skewered him with a sharp stare. "I meant the part where you said that's everything worth knowing about you."

He massaged the center of his chest. "What is this, an inquisition?"

"Give me a break, O'Grady." Golden brown curls shimmered as she gave her head an annoyed toss. "What's wrong with a new friend wanting to get to know you a little better?"

Two friends just chatting. Right. Boy, he could be dense sometimes. "Guess I'm not much into talking about myself."

"I gathered that the day we first met." With a dramatic eye roll, she laid a couple of napkins out, then made six little cracker-and-cheese sandwiches, three on each napkin. She slid one closer to him. "There. Peace offering. I won't ask any more questions. We can sit here quietly and enjoy the afternoon until our jailer returns to set us free."

It sounded like a sensible plan. So why did he want her to keep talking? Keep *asking*? Chewing slowly, he finished one of the cracker sandwiches, then another. Picking up the last one, he stared at it for several seconds, then laid it back down. "I failed," he said. "Failed myself, failed my mission organization, failed God. That's why I'm back here in the States trying to pick up the pieces. Why my brother made me come to Juniper Bluff. Why

Kent is putting me to work on his ranch and why he co-erced me into joining the church's service committee."

Brooke didn't respond right away, which made him wish he'd kept his mouth shut. Talk about oversharing!

Then she tilted her head and smiled. "Was that so hard?"

"Yeah, as a matter of fact. Painfully, ridiculously hard." He grabbed the last cracker sandwich and shoved the whole thing into his mouth. Definitely one way to shut himself up. The cracker sucked all the moisture out of his mouth. Or maybe he could blame his sudden thirst on how Brooke was looking at him. A little bit sad, a little bit worried, a little bit hopeful.

She handed him his soft drink and waited while he sipped. "Why do you feel like you failed?"

He took another swallow of his drink. "Long story short, the more help we provided the church community in Ethiopia, the more dependent they became. Eventually, it felt like we were doing more harm than good."

"Ah." She cast him a meaningful glance. "That explains a lot."

With a guilty grimace, he asked, "How are you so good at reading other people but have trouble looking inside yourself for answers?"

Her tight-lipped frown made him worry he'd gotten a bit too personal, but then she heaved a long, slow sigh. "Blame it on my career in advertising, I guess. Running a successful ad campaign means knowing not only what the buying public will key in on but also what will keep your clients happy."

"And your own happiness?"

She looked away. "There'll be time for that…someday."

Maybe they were more alike than he'd wanted to

admit. How long had he been putting off addressing his own needs while carrying the struggles of the whole world on his shoulders? Replaying his phone call with Henry Voss, he murmured, "What if we're running out of time?"

Time. Brooke closed her eyes. Nothing she'd tried had slowed the relentless march of time as her mother's life ticked away. Every minute since, she'd been running nonstop in a futile effort to outpace her grief.

She scrambled to her feet. Marching to the other side of the oak tree, she strained her eyes for any sign of Kent's return. "Where is he? This is just cruel."

Shaun eased up beside her. He placed a comforting hand on her shoulder. "You have to admit his little stunt did get us talking."

"Maybe. But not about the Christmas outreach." Bristling, she took a giant step forward, then spun around to face him. "Which was why I took an entire afternoon off from work to come out here in the first place."

"Even so, I wouldn't call it a wasted trip." His boyish smile drained away a portion of her annoyance. "Wouldn't you agree we understand each other a little better now?"

Hands tucked into the pockets of her bomber jacket, she shrugged. "I understand we're both operating in avoidance mode. You don't want to talk about your perceived failure in your missions work, and I don't want to talk about how poorly I'm coping with leaving a job I loved, moving back to Texas and facing the holidays without my—"

Her voice broke, and suddenly she was in Shaun's arms. She couldn't say who made the first move, but at the moment it didn't matter. He felt strong and solid and real. Not like the commiserating hugs shared with her father and brother. Not like the consoling embrace from her pastor at Mom's funeral. No, this was different. Like two lost people stretching out their hands through the darkness and finding a fitting companion for the journey.

"Brooke." Shaun's voice was rough with emotion, as if he'd also sensed the *something more* as he held her. "Look. Kent's coming with the horses."

Slipping from his arms, she gave her damp cheeks a quick swipe. The sound of hoofbeats grew louder, and she turned to see Kent riding up.

He eyed them with a questioning grin. "Maybe I should have stayed away a little longer."

Shaun offered Brooke a quick wink. "I'd say you're right on time."

"That was a dirty trick." Brooke tried to look cross, but the memory of Shaun's arms around her stole some of her bravado. She strode over to gather up the remains of their picnic. While she packed the saddlebag, Shaun rolled up the quilt.

Minutes later, they mounted their horses and headed toward the barn. This time, Brooke kept her horse even with Shaun's. It felt nice to share the golden light of late afternoon with him. They might have their disagreements about the Christmas project, but after what they'd just shared—the grief she'd buried deep, his nagging sense of failure—she felt a special kind of closeness with him.

Attraction? Impossible. He was just a really nice guy who was quickly becoming a good friend. That was all it could be, because Brooke wasn't ready for anything more. And the way her life was going, she doubted she'd ever find the courage to let someone new into her heart. Someone she might love…and someday lose.

Two hours later, Brooke sat back and stretched her arms over her head. "I can't believe it. We actually have a plan."

Shaun dropped his pen next to his steno pad. "And it only took eleven days, a few too many heated discussions—"

"And a teensy bit of interference from your annoying future brother-in-law."

From the living room came Kent's good-natured growl, "I heard that!"

An answering growl emanated from somewhere in the area of Shaun's belly. He gave an embarrassed grin. "My cheese and crackers are wearing off."

Aware of her own hunger pangs, Brooke checked the time on her phone. "Oh, no. I was supposed to be home by now. Dad and I were invited to Tripp and Diana's for supper." She'd silenced her phone earlier, and the display indicated two missed calls and a voice mail from her dad's number. "I'd better call and let them know I'm on my way."

While she waited for her father to answer, she shoved everything into her tote. When Dad picked up, he said he was already at Tripp's and that she should come straight there.

Shaun helped her on with her jacket. "Sorry you have to rush off."

She felt the same way, or maybe she only wanted to delay the inevitable conversation with her family about Thanksgiving plans. "What, you aren't sick of me after an entire afternoon of forced proximity?"

"Turned out pretty good, I'd say." He held the door for her as they started out to her car. "Well worth the minor inconvenience."

Darkness had fallen, and Kent's amber-tinged flood-lights cast a surreal glow across the yard. Reaching the car, Brooke set her tote inside, then turned to Shaun. "Guess I'll see you Sunday at church."

"Right." He stepped aside as she slid behind the wheel. "Have a good weekend."

"Thanks. You, too." Weird how they suddenly seemed so formal with each other. The bubbly sensations filling her chest had her utterly confused, and she pondered them all the way to Tripp's house.

Letting herself in through the front door, she inhaled the tempting aroma of savory baked chicken. "I'm here," she called, stepping around one of Diana's cats on her way to the kitchen. "Sorry I ran so late."

"Just sat down." Diana motioned to the empty chair across from her. "Dad's already blessed the food, so help yourself. How'd your meeting go?"

"Pretty well. We now have a solid plan to present to the committee." After spreading a napkin on her lap, Brooke drizzled balsamic dressing over her salad. "This all looks wonderful, Diana."

Dad peered at her. "Looks like you got a little sun today. Outside much?"

"Yes, actually." She served herself some chicken and mixed steamed vegetables. "Kent took us on a trail ride."

"My kind of committee meeting." Tripp reached over to spear a cucumber from Diana's salad plate.

Brooke gasped. "Tripp, that isn't on your diet. How many times—"

Under the table, his foot collided with her shin. Not

hard enough to hurt, but enough to remind her she wasn't the Crohn's police. "Cool it, sis. It's just one bite, and I haven't had a flare-up in months."

"I know, but—" Emotions welling, she squeezed her eyes shut against the image of her brother collapsing from stomach pain after their mother's funeral. He could have died, too, and all because he'd neglected his diet and Crohn's medication. "Somebody in this family has to be responsible, and if you won't take care of yourself—"

"That's enough, Brooke." Her father spoke quietly but firmly as he laid a restraining hand on her arm.

She exhaled sharply. "I'm sorry. I don't know what's wrong with me lately."

"We do," Diana said, her tone warm with empathy. "We all realize how hard this Thanksgiving is going to be, so one of the reasons Tripp and I invited you over tonight was so we could share an idea we had."

"I thought it was all settled."

"My parents extended the invitation, yes. But they'll completely understand if we decide to do something different." Diana shared a smile with Tripp. "So here's our idea. At the assisted living center where my great-aunt Jennie lives, many of the residents don't have family nearby. What if, instead of going out to my parents' for a traditional family Thanksgiving, we all have dinner at the center? Then afterward, my Visiting Pet Pals group could stop in with animals to cuddle. Bringing a little Thanksgiving cheer to some lonely old folks could be a special way to honor your mom's memory."

Brooke let the suggestion sink in for a moment. She cast her dad a questioning glance. "Are you okay with this?"

Eyes misty, he nodded. "More'n okay."

It wasn't an escape to the coast, and the memories would still linger near, but she couldn't argue the fact that her mother would have absolutely loved the idea of sharing her favorite holiday in this way. "Then let's do it. Thank you, Diana." She released a shaky laugh. "Makes me wish I had a pet so I could join your group."

"No worries. You can borrow one of mine. I'll be bringing Alice—" Diana's brown-spotted lop-eared rabbit "—but you could be in charge of Ginger."

Ginger was Aunt Jennie's feisty little corgi that Diana and Tripp had adopted. Brooke nodded. "I'd love to."

Tripp slid his chair back. "And while we've been talking pet pals and holiday plans, our food's gotten cold. Hand me your plates. I'll pop them in the microwave for a quick warmup."

Later, when Tripp volunteered to wash dishes, Brooke offered to help. As he handed her a plate to set in the dishwasher, she looked up at him with a penitent smile. "Sorry again about getting on your case earlier."

"You worry. I get it." He rested an elbow on the counter, which brought him closer to her level. "You've invested so much of yourself in looking after everyone else in the family—making sure Mom had all the best care, trying to keep Dad's spirits up." He rolled his eyes. "And scrutinizing every morsel that goes into my mouth like a fussy mama bird."

Wincing, she ducked her head. "I think that last part may be a slight exaggeration."

"I just want you to stop being so hard on yourself. We all know moving back to Texas wasn't what you wanted, and if I put any extra pressure on you about bringing Dad here, I apologize."

She reached for another plate. "Mom and Dad never

truly felt at home in California. Now that Mom's gone, this is where he needs to be."

"But what about you? Is this where *you* need to be?"

It was a question she'd asked herself again and again over the last several weeks. "For now, anyway."

But who knew what the future held? If her father really was ready to move on, possibly remarry someday, she didn't think she could stick around to watch that happen. Besides, her former boss at the advertising firm had told her if she ever moved back to LA, she'd always have a place in the company.

For now, she could only take things day by day, controlling what she could so she'd be ready for whatever tomorrow might bring.

Chapter Eight

More times than he could count over the weekend, Shaun found himself thinking of Brooke. They'd definitely turned a corner in their friendship on Friday. What exactly lay around that corner remained to be seen.

The meaningful grins he kept getting from Kent didn't help.

And neither did the all-too-brief smile Brooke had given him across the church sanctuary Sunday morning, almost as if she'd rather not have acknowledged him at all.

They needed to touch base before the committee meeting, though. On Monday afternoon, he phoned her cell and hoped he wasn't catching her in the middle of pressing chamber of commerce business.

"Hi, Shaun. I was just about to call you." She'd slipped into her professional persona. "Would you mind if I take the lead tonight when we outline our plan of action?"

"Uh, that's fine."

"I mean, since I have all the notes on my computer, I've been organizing our list of tasks so it'll be easier to distribute jobs to each of the members."

"Makes sense." He paused a beat to ask himself why he was needed at the meeting at all. "Guess I'll see you there."

"Seven o'clock. And I'll arrive a few minutes early to make sure everything's in order."

He had no doubt. "Brooke…is everything okay?"

"Of course." The forced smile was evident in her tone. "I've just had a lot on my mind, and I want everything to go well this evening." Another phone rang close by. "I need to get that. See you later, Shaun. Bye!"

What happened to the closeness they'd shared only three days ago as they'd celebrated finalizing their proposal for the Christmas outreach? Had he only imagined the spark between them? Because something about Brooke Willoughby had set loose all kinds of thoughts he'd been suppressing for the last few years. Thoughts of letting someone new into his heart. Thoughts of putting down roots and starting a family of his own.

Is this what You've been trying to tell me, Lord? Is it time to retire from missions work?

His only answer was the sound of laughter from the living room, where Kent and Erin had been going over wedding details for the past hour or two. Although he suspected there'd been more kissing than talking involved. Good thing the wedding was less than three weeks away.

Which reminded him of something else he'd been pondering. He ambled into the living room. "Hey, you two. Sounds like you need a chaperone."

Erin and Kent sprang to opposite ends of the sofa, the wedding planning notebook obviously forgotten where it lay on the floor.

"Probably right about that," Kent said with an embarrassed grin.

Her face a bright shade of pink, Erin snatched up the

notebook and frantically flipped pages. "We were just going over the menu for the rehearsal dinner. Kent, you should call your mom and make sure we've included everyone."

Kent's brow furrowed. "Uh, didn't she just email us a list last week?"

"I know, but—"

"It's okay, little sis. There's no law against kissing your fiancé." With a snicker, Shaun took a seat in the antique wooden rocking chair Erin had recently added to the room's country-style decor. "But while you're taking a break from, uh, whatever... I mean, if you'd still like me to take part in the ceremony—"

Erin leaped from the sofa and threw her arms around his neck. "Oh, Shaun, you'll marry us? I'm so glad!"

Sputtering a laugh, he brushed her auburn curls out of his mouth. "I won't be much use if you strangle me first!"

She loosened her hold enough to kiss him on the cheek, then drew back to her spot on the sofa next to Kent. "We can't thank you enough, but...what made you change your mind?"

"I could say you finally wore me down with your pestering, but that wouldn't be entirely true." He glanced toward their engagement portrait on Kent's fireplace mantel. Their loving expressions in the photograph had been tugging at his heart ever since Erin had first emailed him a copy last summer with the news of her upcoming wedding. "Consider it my gift to a couple who's very, very dear to me."

Kent reached over to grip Shaun's hand. "Whatever convinced you, we're mighty grateful. This means a lot to both of us."

"Means a lot to me, too." Before things turned any

more maudlin, Shaun rose to excuse himself. "I'll let you get back to your wedding planning." With a wink and a smile, he paused at the recliner to give Skip a pat. "Help me keep an eye on these two, you hear?"

The old dog barely lifted his head, then went right back to doggy dreamland.

Erin left a short time later to pick up Avery from school, and Kent enlisted Shaun to help him with a few barn chores before supper. He was getting pretty good at mucking stalls, stacking hay bales and measuring out feed, for all the good it would do him wherever God took him next. It completely baffled him that he could suddenly experience such clarity about agreeing to officiate at his sister's wedding and still not sense any confirmation from the Lord about returning to Jordan.

Or maybe it wasn't so hard to understand after all. He'd come to realize that the blessing of Erin and Kent's marriage would be totally God's doing and not dependent on his struggling faith.

At least he knew where he was supposed to be for the holiday season. Between his sister's wedding, the Christmas service project and helping Kent around the ranch, he wouldn't lack for ways to keep occupied.

After supper, he and Kent headed to the church. He spotted Brooke's little red car parked near the entrance to the Sunday school wing, and Kent pulled his pickup in next to it. Inside the building, animated voices echoed from the meeting room. Sounded like Brooke was already describing their plans to Emily.

"I love it, just love it!" Emily exclaimed as Shaun and Kent ambled into the room. "Oh, Shaun. I knew I could count on you and Brooke. I can't wait for us to get started."

"When we heard about the needs at the mobile home park, the rest was easy." He cast Brooke a wry smile.

She smiled back, one brow arched provocatively. "Oh, yes, after our visit out there, we just breezed right through the planning process."

Kent snickered as he pulled out a chair. "I can certainly vouch for that."

Memories of being stranded with Brooke last Friday brought a twinge to Shaun's gut, along with the sense that whatever God had in store for him, she was part of it. Could her role in his future extend beyond the Christmas outreach? He couldn't imagine how, because there was no way he could picture prim and proper Brooke Willoughby on the mission field.

Brooke couldn't fully explain her new awkwardness around Shaun. It wasn't like they were romantically involved—which they never would be, considering he'd probably leave again for the mission field after Christmas. Besides, since Friday she'd begun entertaining thoughts about eventually moving back to California. She'd stay long enough to make sure Dad was settled and content. With Tripp and Diana living just up the street, he'd be well looked after.

When most of the committee members had arrived, Emily called the meeting to order. "Let's get right to our Christmas outreach. Brooke and Shaun have put together an excellent service project with multiple phases. I'll let them tell you all about it."

Brooke distributed the printed copies of the task list she'd put together. "Are any of you familiar with the Whitetail Valley Mobile Home Park?" After a few nods in response, she went on, "Shaun and I visited with the manager last week and met a few of the residents, many of whom are immigrants with limited financial resources." She described some of their observations and how Mr. Zamora strove to provide what amenities he could while keeping rent affordable. "We've come up with several things our church can do, not only to bless these families at Christmas but to make their lives better going forward."

The silver-haired woman at the other end of the table spoke up. "This is quite a list. I'm a bit concerned we'll be biting off more than we can chew."

Brooke remembered the woman had had a lot to say at the previous meeting as well. "Forgive me, I don't remember your name."

"Alma Cox." Alma tapped a cherry red fingernail against the printout. "I'm seventy-four years old, and I can't see myself painting a recreation hall or fixing potholes in a driveway."

"And you certainly wouldn't be expected to." Brooke smiled indulgently. "I'm sure we'll find something much more in line with your...talents." Which she hoped included abilities much more productive than pointing out the cloud in every silver lining.

"I can help with the painting," Kent volunteered. "Pretty sure I can wrangle a donation of supplies from my boss at Zipp's Hardware. I'd be happy to take a look at those broken washing machines, too."

"Great, thank you!" Glancing across the table, she noticed Shaun sitting quietly, hands folded. Had she been too pushy about assuming control of the meeting? "Um, Shaun, would you like to take it from here?"

His lips twitched in a semblance of a smile. "That's okay. You're doing fine."

Then why didn't it *feel* fine? She fumbled to find

her place in her notes. "That brings us to the Christmas shop. We need volunteers to solicit donations of clothing, household items, toys and also nonperishable food items. We'll hold the shop in the church fellowship hall the Saturday before Christmas, and the park residents will be given vouchers they can use to 'buy' gifts and groceries for their families."

Alma Cox said she could make some calls for donations, which seemed appropriate since obviously the woman was rarely at a loss for words—provided her brusque nature didn't offend potential donors. After elaborating on a few more items on the task list, Brooke passed around a signup sheet. By the time it made its way around the table and back to her, she released an inward sigh of relief to see that most of the slots had been filled, including the next few Saturdays as workdays for repairs and renovations at the mobile home park.

Emily consulted her calendar. "All right, everyone, we have a lot to do between now and Christmas. We'll keep in touch via phone and email over the next few weeks, and I'd also like us to meet every other Monday for progress reports. Are we all in agreement?"

With no dissensions, she adjourned the meeting. As the members filed out, she drew Brooke and Shaun aside. "Wonderful, wonderful job, you two! I knew I'd made the right choice when I paired you up on this project."

"I'm just glad we were able to pull together a plan that everyone seems happy with." *Alma Cox aside*, Brooke didn't add. "If Alan Glazer hadn't been at the chamber of commerce last week…" No need to let on about the endless arguments she and Shaun had gotten into while trying to come to consensus. She cast him an uneasy smile.

"I mean, getting the perspective of someone with a direct connection to the situation made a huge difference."

"That's one of the nicest things about living in a small town," Emily said as she pushed chairs in and turned off lights. "No matter what your occupation, it's never *just business*. It's family. And families always try to help wherever there's a need."

Unless your family decides they don't need or want your help. Brooke couldn't stop her thoughts from returning to Friday night, when Tripp had plainly let her know he didn't appreciate her micromanaging his Crohn's diet. Then there was the whole thing with Dad and his new lady friend from church. Didn't she have only their best interests at heart?

In the parking lot, Shaun paused next to Brooke near the front of Kent's pickup. He waited until Kent had climbed in behind the wheel, then turned slowly to face Brooke. "Have I done something to get on your bad side?"

She jerked her chin back. "If this is about me doing all the talking tonight, I was only trying to keep us on track. You know how quickly committee discussions can drift off topic."

"If you're sure that's all it is." His shrug and sidelong glance said he wasn't convinced.

"I wasn't intentionally shutting you out, Shaun, I promise." She took a tentative step toward him, then hugged her tote against her chest and backed away. "I just operate better when I can keep things professional."

"So...none of this is personal for you? Even after what we saw at the mobile home park? After everything we said we wanted to do for those families?"

He was reading her all wrong. "Yes, it's personal." *Too* personal, maybe. How could she explain the complicated and completely out-of-control thoughts racing through her head? "I care as much as you do about the families out there. Why do you think I've invested so much effort into making sure everything goes perfectly?"

"I don't know, Brooke. Why *are* you so invested in this project? Because, as I recall, you were as unwilling to get involved as I was in the beginning."

"Well, it's…it's important to help people in our community. Besides, my boss thinks it'll help me develop business relationships and—"

"Your *boss* thinks it's a good idea? So ultimately it's about what benefits you and your job." Shaun raised both hands in a gesture of disgust and started toward the pickup. "Good night, Brooke. See you Saturday at the workday."

She stood there with her mouth hanging open while Kent backed out of the parking space and drove away. How had she messed this up so horribly? She'd give anything to be able to turn back the clock—better yet, flip backward through the entire calendar. Wouldn't it be nice if one of those angelic characters from a sentimental made-for-TV Christmas movie would suddenly appear and offer her a do-over of the last five years or so? With hindsight to guide her, she could have made sure Mom got treatment much sooner for her kidney disease. They could have worked even harder to find a donor and saved Mom's life.

And with both her parents happy and healthy, she could still be working at a top-notch advertising firm and thriving in the accounts management position she'd aspired to all through college. True, Los Angeles hadn't originally been her top choice of places to live. Also true that one of the reasons she'd moved there in the first place was because of her then-boyfriend and the future she'd envisioned sharing with him as they'd climbed the advertising career ladder together.

Well, the boyfriend was no more—turned out he was more in love with success than with her—but the ultra-big-city whirlwind of activity had grown on her. Her job here at the Juniper Bluff Chamber of Commerce felt like…failing? No, the job itself had its merits. It just wasn't how she'd envisioned her professional life unfolding.

You've lost control, Brooke. Why not admit it?

Because that *would* be failing, and failure was one word she'd studiously omitted from her vocabulary.

Why did he feel like he'd failed…again? Walking away like that, leaving things unsettled between them— that wasn't how Shaun typically handled things. Until he met Brooke, anyway.

Or maybe it began when he'd bailed on the Ethiopia mission. He'd failed there, too, even though Henry Voss had done everything possible to assure him otherwise. *You accomplished what you were sent to do,* Henry had told him. *It was time to let the church there find its own footing. Now you need to find yours.*

Easier said than done.

"Earth to Shaun." Kent reached across the truck cab to tap him on the arm. "You hardly said three words at the meeting. Something happen between you and Brooke?"

"You're asking the wrong person."

"Something's obviously going on. The looks you two were giving each other in the parking lot just now?" Kent whistled through his teeth. "A whole lot different from how y'all were acting when she left the ranch last Friday."

Friday already seemed like a lifetime ago. "You know

the proverbial oil-and-water thing? Guess that's Brooke and me."

"I'm thinkin' more like matches and kerosene. There's definitely a spark between you two."

"And you know what they say about playing with fire." These metaphors were getting a little too corny. Not to mention Kent's observations were way off base. "All I care about right now is getting through Christmas and getting on with my life."

Kent snorted. "I'll try not to be offended you seem in such a hurry to skip right past your sister's wedding."

"Didn't mean it that way." Squinting to avoid an oncoming vehicle's bright headlights, Shaun massaged the bridge of his nose. "Fact is, I'm as confused as you are about the way Brooke was acting tonight. I kept asking her—asking myself—if I'd done or said anything to change things between us."

But maybe that was the whole issue. There *wasn't* anything between them, or at least there shouldn't be. At this point, Shaun had every intention of letting Henry Voss know he was on board with the new missionary post in Jordan. It would be good to get back in familiar territory. Even more important, this call meshed perfectly with his gifts and skills. It was a no-brainer.

Kent had gone silent as he pulled in at the ranch. He shut off the engine, then rested his hands on his knees. Shaun had the feeling he should stay in his seat while his future brother-in-law said whatever was on his mind.

"I wouldn't presume to tell you how to run your life," Kent began. "The Lord knows exactly how long it took me to get my own life back on track after I'd drifted so far from Him. Raising my cattle, working at the hardware store, living life on my terms—I thought I was content, but turns out something real important was missing. I just didn't know what it was until I met Erin."

"If you're trying to tell me I need a woman in my life—that maybe that woman is Brooke Willoughby—you couldn't be more wrong. For one thing, we have zero in common. For another, I'll be leaving for Jordan in January."

"Jordan?" Kent's head jerked around. "When did you decide that?"

Shaun could kick himself for saying anything until after he'd confirmed the arrangements with Henry. "The position's been on the table for a couple of weeks. I needed time to think and pray about it."

"Have you told Erin yet?"

"I will…when the time is right. She has plenty on her plate right now with wedding plans."

Kent laughed sharply. "Excuse me, but that sounds like a cop-out."

"Just because you're marrying my sister doesn't give you the right to pass judgment on my personal decisions." Shaun thrust open the door, only to be blasted by a gust of wintry air. Guess the predicted cold front had finally blown in, though it hardly compared with the chill inside Kent's truck.

As he marched toward the house, Kent's boots pounded the ground behind him. "Shaun, hold up."

Halting outside the back porch, he spun around. "Why? So you can deliver more of your homegrown country-style wisdom?" Then, hearing the bitterness in his tone, he whooshed out a breath. "Sorry, man. I know you're trying to help. But it's the kind of help I don't need right now."

Kent rested his fists low on his hips. "Sure about that?"

Head lowered, Shaun looked away. "No."

"That's what I thought." Kent brushed past him and led the way inside. "Feel like some decaf?" He was already measuring water into the coffee maker.

Ten minutes later, they sat at the kitchen table with steaming mugs and buttered slabs of the banana bread Kent said Erin had dropped off for him at the hardware store that morning.

"So you're set on going back overseas," Kent stated. "You said you prayed about it. Did God answer?"

"It just makes sense." Shaun took a slow sip of coffee. "One of the few things that does anymore."

"Making sense isn't necessarily an answer. Did it make sense for God to come to earth as a baby? Did it make sense for Jesus to die on a cross?"

A feeble grin teased the corners of Shaun's mouth. "You're preaching to the choir, brother."

"Last I checked, being in the choir doesn't mean you have everything all figured out."

"True enough." Shaun studied a forkful of banana bread. "Okay, maybe I haven't heard directly from God about accepting this Jordan assignment. But He hasn't given me a firm no, either. And since I've always believed God expects us to keep moving forward on the part of the path we can see, that's what I'm doing. If and when He puts up a roadblock or detour sign, then I'll change course."

Later, standing at the bathroom mirror to brush his teeth, he kept seeing Brooke's face just before he'd left her standing on the curb in front of the church. And superimposed over the image was a flashing neon sign: *Caution! Major detour ahead!*

Chapter Nine

Now that the specifics of the Christmas outreach project had been assigned to various committee members, Brooke felt the pressure begin to lift. For the rest of the week, she made a concerted effort to keep her attention on chamber of commerce business while trying hard not to think about how Shaun had turned his back on her Monday night.

So what if she'd exercised a little professional command at the meeting? Wasn't that her forte? Wasn't it a key reason Emily had pigeonholed her for this project in the first place? And as far as her boss endorsing her involvement with the committee, Shaun shouldn't be upset about local businesspeople wanting to help those in need.

Then Saturday rolled around, and the idea of facing Shaun again made her stomach feel like the inside of the turbo-speed food chopper she'd created a successful ad campaign for last year. At least it wouldn't be just the two of them. In addition to the committee members who'd signed up for the first workday, Dad said he'd like to come along, and Tripp and Diana both promised to get there as soon as their Saturday-morning work schedules allowed.

On the other hand, considering how her family continually nagged her about her social life, or rather lack thereof, being subjected to their play-by-play commentary as she interacted with Shaun might prove the greater risk.

Hair pulled up in a ponytail, and dressed in her scruffiest jeans, sweatshirt and sneakers, she arrived with her father at Whitetail Valley Mobile Home Park shortly after 8:00 a.m. on Saturday. Shaun's rattletrap car wasn't anywhere in sight, and neither was Kent's truck. Good, a few more minutes to compose herself.

Mr. Zamora bustled out of the office to greet them. "Welcome. Everyone here has been so excited about today, and a few of our residents are also available to pitch in."

"That's great. And the weather is cooperating, too," Brooke said with a glance toward the cloudless sky. She introduced her dad, and the men shook hands. "The plan is to get started painting the rec hall this morning. Also, one of our committee members is a handyman who said he'd take a look at those broken washing machines."

Just then, the rumble of an out-of-tune engine drew her attention, and Shaun's old green car pulled up. Climbing out, he took exaggerated care in making sure his car door didn't nick hers.

"Good morning," he called, zipping up his fleece-lined flannel jacket. He popped open the back of his car. "I have all the painting supplies, compliments of Zipp's Hardware, thanks to Kent." More volunteers drove up as he spoke. "I can get the crew started…" A sardonic grin curled one side of his mouth as he nodded toward Brooke. "Unless you'd rather take the lead."

"You go right ahead." She hadn't been looking forward to ruining her clothes and hair with paint spatters. "I think I'll help with the grounds cleanup." She did know a thing or two about gardening, an interest she'd developed while puttering around her little house in LA. Shoving down a twinge of homesickness, she turned to her dad. "Want to pull some weeds with me?"

Her father frowned as he massaged his lower back. "Gettin' a bit too old for all that bending and stooping. Think I'll join the painting crew."

Since when had her dad developed back problems? He never seemed to have any trouble scooping up a tennis ball to play fetch with Ginger in Tripp's backyard. And wasn't this the same guy who kept insisting Brooke didn't need to hire a housekeeper or lawn service because he was perfectly capable of doing the vacuuming and yard work?

Emily Ingram strode over with a pair of gardening gloves and a box of trash bags. "Where shall we start, Brooke?"

She forced a smile. At least she had one person willing to work alongside her. "How about the park office entrance? I'm a firm believer in the power of positive first impressions."

On the other hand, recent experience had shown her that later impressions typically revealed the real truth. Hadn't Shaun seemed nice enough the day she'd first met him at Diana's Donuts? Even after Emily had drafted them for this project, she'd thought they might actually get along. If only she'd known then what she knew now about the man's bristly character.

Look who's talking. She was the one who'd broken the accord they'd reached at their last planning meeting out at Kent's ranch. As for taking the lead at the committee meeting, if Shaun really believed she'd meant to crowd him out, she owed him an apology.

Emily dropped to her knees beneath the park office window and began tugging at weeds. "This would be a perfect spot for a couple of rosebushes, don't you think? I love roses."

Pulling a trash bag from the box, Brooke peeled it open, then gathered up the pile Emily had started. "Roses take a lot of care. I'd suggest low-maintenance shrubs, like hollies or boxwoods—" *There you go again, pushing for your own way.* She drew a quick breath. "You're right, though. Roses would really brighten things up, and they'd smell so good, too."

A couple of other ladies from the committee joined them with hand trowels and spades, and soon they'd cleared a two-foot-wide stretch along either side of the office entrance. One of them mentioned having several yards of plastic edging left over from a home garden project and offered to bring it next time. "I can also make some cuttings from some of my hardier plants," she added.

Emily stood and brushed the soil off her knees. "I need to run errands in Fredericksburg next week. I'll stop by the discount garden center and look at their rosebushes. Maybe I can even wrangle a donation from them."

Men's laughter drew Brooke's attention. Stepping around the building, she glimpsed Shaun and the painting crew striding over from the rec hall. Shaun had shed his jacket, and now his denim baseball cap, long-sleeved

T-shirt and jeans bore several splotches of eggshell white. The rest of his group didn't look much better, including Brooke's father, who looked as if he'd dipped his entire right arm in a paint bucket.

Unable to resist a smile, she shook her head. "I thought y'all were painting walls, not each other."

The moment their gazes met, the change in Shaun's expression sent a shiver up her spine. His tone turned mellow as he said, "I can guarantee the rec hall looks a lot better than we do."

"That's a relief." The sarcasm she'd tried for didn't quite come through. "Are you finished already?"

"First coat. It's past noon, and we're all getting hungry."

"Is it that late already?" Brooke tugged her phone from her hoodie pocket to check the time. "Lunch should be here any minute." The supermarket deli manager had agreed to donate box lunches for today's volunteers, and Diana and Tripp would be bringing them out.

They drove up not five seconds later. The volunteers swarmed Tripp's SUV and carried the meals over to the folding tables Mr. Zamora had set up outside the rec hall. Mrs. Paulos and Mrs. Tran, the ladies Brooke had met when she and Shaun had first visited the park, served fresh-brewed coffee and iced tea.

For dessert, Mrs. Paulos had baked a big batch of delightful-smelling date cookies she called *maamoul*. Diana raved about them, claiming she could sell them by the dozens at the doughnut shop if the woman might be willing to share the recipe. "I'd even hire you to bake them in my shop once or twice a week."

Mrs. Paulos's face lit up. "I must first ask my husband, of course, but it would be my pleasure."

Shaun ambled over to where Brooke stood, her fingers soaking up the warmth from a hot cup of coffee. He nodded toward the beaming Mrs. Paulos, who'd rushed over to speak to her husband. "See? We're already making a lasting difference here."

"That's what you wanted all along, isn't it?" She hoped her tone hadn't come across as snippy as it sounded to her own ears. "I mean, you were right. It feels good to be a part of something that will help these families for more than a day."

He grew quiet for a moment as they stood watching the volunteers and residents enjoying food and conversation under a sun-drenched November sky. "I'm not exactly sure where we got off track this week. I wish you'd tell me how to fix it."

"Neither of us did anything wrong, Shaun. We were both trying to do something good. We just had strong ideas on what was best." She set her coffee cup on a nearby table and offered a hesitant smile. "And, as you may have noticed, I have some control issues."

"Uh, yeah. Got a few of my own, obviously." He snickered softly, but there was no derision in his expression. "Need to talk about it?"

It might be good to talk things over with someone who could be a little more objective than her dad, brother or nosy best-friend-slash-sister-in-law. "Are you offering in your capacity as a pastor?"

"If that's what you want, sure. But I'd like it a lot better if you could think of me as a friend."

"I haven't had many of those since college. Not real friends, anyway. Guess I was too busy climbing the career ladder." Looking skyward, she snorted a laugh. "Does that make me sound pathetic or what?"

"It makes you sound like someone who knows what she wants and goes after it."

"But at the expense of my relationships?" Why did her eyes suddenly prick with tears? "I've been telling my dad how to run his life, I've been nagging my brother about his dietary habits, and now I've managed to mess things up with you."

"You haven't messed anything up, Brooke." With a glance toward the others, Shaun led her a little distance away. "Look at all the good we're doing here. This wouldn't be happening if you weren't so—"

"Pushy? Domineering?" She narrowed one eye.

"I was going to say confident and determined. You certainly knew how to keep me from digging in my heels with my stubborn idealism."

His words elicited a chuckle. "That's what you're calling it? I would have described it as stiff-necked obstinacy."

Doubling over as if he'd just been socked in the stomach, he groaned. "Low blow."

"I concede, that might have been a slight exaggeration." She released a sigh. "We're a pair, aren't we?"

"I'll say." Shaun sobered, his gaze melding with hers. He slowly lifted his hand and drew a fingertip beneath her lower lids to brush away a trace of wetness.

His touch froze her to the spot. Her glance dipped to his lips, and she had the craziest longing to kiss him.

"There you two are." Emily Ingram's face appeared over Shaun's shoulder. "Everyone's ready to get back to work, but we need our generals to give the order."

Generals? Giving orders? If anything could snap Brooke out of her unexpected and utterly unwelcome thoughts of romance, Emily's choice of words certainly did the trick.

* * *

Close call, O'Grady. Way too close. If Emily Ingram hadn't come along at precisely that moment, Shaun wasn't sure he could have resisted the impulse to kiss Brooke. And the look in her eyes had told him she'd felt it, too.

Then he'd seen her wince at Emily's use of the word *general*, and his heart about snapped. The woman was struggling, that much was clear. Ten more minutes alone with her during Kent's "forced proximity" ploy the other day, and she might have revealed more about the things that troubled her.

Oh, well, time to get started on the second coat of paint in the rec hall. Maybe this afternoon he could arrange to work on the other side of the room from Brooke's father. The man was nice enough, but his overprotective streak came through loud and clear. All morning long, he'd plied Shaun with ambiguously worded questions disguised as friendly getting-to-know-each-other conversation. Where had Shaun grown up? Had he always wanted to be a missionary? Any marital aspirations? Where did he see himself in the next five years?

In other words, *What are your intentions toward my daughter?*

He should have come right out and told the man there was no chance of anything between him and Brooke. Shaun would soon be on a plane to the Middle East, and Brooke…

No, it wasn't his place to suggest to her father that she didn't seem happy in Juniper Bluff, nor that he suspected she might decide to head back to LA first chance she got.

It wasn't Shaun's place to care one way or the other. So why did he? What was it about Brooke Willoughby that continually flashed those *Caution! Detour!* signs he was determined to ignore?

"There you are, Shaun." Kent found him behind the rec building as he stalled longer than necessary stirring a paint can. "Sorry I couldn't get here sooner. Looks like things are humming along."

"It's going well." Straightening, Shaun used an old rag to wipe a dribble of paint off his hand. "Have you had a chance to check out those washing machines?"

"That's what I was coming out to tell you. They're definitely fixable, but I'd have to order some parts." He grimaced. "It'll run a lot less than buying new appliances, but it won't be cheap. Before I place the order, you should check with Emily to see if there's room in the committee's budget."

Shaun nodded. He knew how it worked in situations like this, but these families needed their laundry facilities. "Go ahead and order the parts, and we'll cover the amount one way or another." Even if he had to dig into his own savings to make up the difference.

"Will do. Wish I could stick around longer, but Erin reminded me we'd scheduled another premarital counseling session with Pastor Terry this afternoon." He blew out through pursed lips. "I am beyond ready to get past all this wedding to-do and get on with the happily married part."

"Two more weeks and you're there." Shaun clapped Kent on the shoulder. "I mean this sincerely—the Lord couldn't have sent a better man into my sister's life. You're going to be a great husband and father."

"Thanks. Wasn't so long ago that I doubted I'd ever be worthy of a wife and family." Kent roughly cleared his throat. "All righty, then. I'll get those parts ordered and hopefully have the washers back in service by next weekend."

Watching his future brother-in-law jog toward the rec building entrance, Shaun shook off his own muddled thoughts about someday starting a family. His brother, Greg, now a widower, already had a daughter in college. His sister, married once before, albeit to a total loser, was raising a precious seven-year-old who had both her uncles and her stepdad-to-be wrapped around her little finger. Shaun enjoyed being an uncle, at least for as much time as he'd gotten to spend with his nieces over the years, but the idea of fatherhood—of bringing a child into his nomadic missionary lifestyle—would it even be fair?

Sure, he knew plenty of missionary families who served all over the world with their children in tow. And the kids grew up more cosmopolitan, more adaptable and more personable than the kids he'd encountered here in the States who couldn't seem to get their heads out of their smartphones long enough to carry on a genuine conversation.

"Get over yourself," he muttered as he hefted the paint can. No point in thinking about fatherhood until he got past the part where he fell in love with the right woman.

Then, rounding the corner, he plowed smack into Brooke on her way out of the rec building. The lid popped off the paint can, and eggshell white ran in oozing rivulets from her knees down to her sneakers.

She shrieked, hands raised in shock.

"Brooke, I'm so sorry!" Shaun set down the can and scanned his surroundings for anything he could use to mop up the mess. Not finding anything, he dropped to his haunches and began using his shirttail to wipe away the paint but only made it worse.

"Stop, okay? It's useless." A tremor laced her tone, and he worried she was about to cry again. Then another sound bubbled up from her chest—laughter. It was possibly the sweetest sound he'd ever heard. "I can't believe I honestly thought I could get through the entire day unscathed. At least now I have another excuse to go shopping."

"Glad to oblige." He stretched out his arms to examine the mess he'd made of his shirt. "I may be in need of a shopping trip, myself."

"If you need a personal shopper, you can always call." She offered a wry, almost apologetic grin. "But if you think I'm bossy now, you should see the damage I could do as your fashion consultant."

Nice to see her lighten up a bit. "I won't deny my wardrobe could use an overhaul. Kent's been trying to talk me into getting fitted for a tux for his wedding. I told him my one and only gray suit would have to do."

"Oh, but you'd look so handsome in a—" Face reddening, Brooke pulled her lips between her teeth.

Heat infused Shaun's face, too, even as his chest swelled at the compliment. Before he realized he was going to ask, he blurted, "I was thinking, I don't have a plus-one for the ceremony. Any chance you'd save me from going stag?"

Her eyelids fluttered. "Wow. Wasn't expecting that."

"Just thought it would be more fun to attend with a friend, especially since we're both fairly new to town and probably won't…" He let the thought fade away.

"Yeah." The word came out on a sigh. She tucked her fingertips into her jeans pockets. "I'd love to attend the wedding with you. Thanks."

"One other thing I should mention, though. Erin and

Kent talked me into co-officiating, so I'll be up front during the actual ceremony." He grinned shyly. "However, my prestigious pastoral role allows me to guarantee you one of the best seats in the house, both at the ceremony and at the reception."

"Now I really must go shopping."

He thought she looked beautiful just as she was, paint-soaked jeans and all, and was about to tell her so before he abruptly came to his senses. Had he really been about to resort to shameless flirting? Because, seriously, this could go nowhere.

Nowhere.

Chapter Ten

One negative about accepting Shaun's invitation to his sister's wedding—it effectively assured she'd have to stick around for Thanksgiving weekend. Since agreeing to Diana's suggestion to have Thanksgiving dinner at her great-aunt's assisted living center, Brooke had been entertaining second thoughts. Even with everyone else around, most of them complete strangers, it would still be a family dinner of sorts.

And Mom wouldn't be there.

Working at her computer Monday morning, she glimpsed a tiny fleck of paint stuck to her pinky finger. With all the scrubbing she'd done since Saturday, how had she missed it? Her paint-soaked jeans and sneakers had gone straight into the trash, even as she'd chuckled again over both her own and Shaun's klutziness. At least he hadn't tried to "dance" with her as he'd done when they'd run into each other in the town square that first day.

Although…would there be dancing at Erin and Kent's wedding? It might be interesting to find out if Shaun O'Grady was any more coordinated on a real dance floor. He certainly had a nice singing voice. She'd sat three rows in front of him in church yesterday and had stopped singing herself long enough to glance around for the fantastic baritone. When they made eye contact, his easy smile had shot a tingle up her spine—and it was happening all over again just thinking about him.

Really, Brooke? Where is your head these days? Obviously not where it needed to be, which currently was updating the chamber's website calendar. Had she actually just typed "*Lose* the Thanksgiving holiday" instead of "*Closed for…*"? Hello, Freudian slip.

With a huff, she backspaced and made the correction. Before she could move on to the next date, her cell phone vibrated on the corner of the desk. A glance at the display evoked an entirely different kind of adrenaline rush. "Zach? Hi!"

"How are you, Brooke?" Her former boss sounded his usual mile-a-minute self. "I'd hoped to hear from you before now. Bored with small-town Texas yet?"

She slipped around her desk to ease her door shut. "It's an adjustment, I admit. How's it going there?"

"Your former accounts keep asking about you. Jeff's trying to pick up the slack, but…" He lowered his voice, and the click of another door closing sounded through the phone. "He'll never match your client rapport, much less your ability to intuit exactly the right angle for each campaign."

"I'm flattered, Zach." Her ex-boyfriend, Jeff, was one thing she did not miss about LA. The rivalry between them, which he'd mostly created, had played a big role in their breakup.

Zach's tone became wheedling. "Flattered enough to come back?"

"Don't think I haven't thought about it." She heaved

a regretful sigh. "But this is where I need to be, at least for now."

"I get it. Your family needs you. How is your dad, by the way?"

"He's doing well." Better than she was, judging from his blossoming friendship with Lydia. Hence the reason he'd asked Brooke to sit farther toward the front of church yesterday, so they could join Lydia and her son who'd arrived for a visit.

The office intercom buzzed on her desk phone. "I hate to cut this short, but my boss needs me. It was great to hear from you, though."

"Call me sometime. And anytime you're ready to come back—"

"I appreciate it." *More than you know.* Ending the call, she shook off the cloud of regret before picking up the intercom. "I'm here, Inez. Sorry, I was on a personal call."

"Just reminding you about our lunch meeting with the mayor. We'll need to leave soon."

Where had the time gone? Not nearly as much to the work at hand as she needed. She'd have to do better this afternoon. "Be right out."

The meeting went well, with plenty of business on the agenda to keep Brooke's thoughts centered on work and not on Shaun, the dreaded Thanksgiving holiday, the Christmas outreach or how badly she wished she could turn her back on all the complications here and catch the next flight to LA.

The rest of the week hummed along pretty much the same. In between chamber business, Brooke fielded regular calls from Alma Cox, who was doing an excellent job of soliciting donations for the Christmas store. Not only had she received commitments from Juniper Bluff merchants but also several in nearby Fredericksburg, Kerrville and Comfort. In addition to the personal wish lists submitted by the Whitetail Valley Mobile Home Park families, they'd have an expansive choice of other gift items, plus nonperishable foods to help stock their pantries.

Shaun called midweek to touch base and asked if they could get together soon to plan out the tasks for the Saturday workday coming up. They agreed to meet at Diana's Donuts at nine thirty Friday morning. Thinking she'd surprise him and be early for a change, she breezed in the door at nine fifteen, only to find him already holding a corner table.

"Mr. Early Bird strikes again," she said, dropping her tote onto an empty chair. "Did you spend the night here or something?"

He twitched a brow. "Or something. I had to be at the tailor's for a suit fitting first thing this morning."

"A tux, perchance?"

"Uh, no. When I pulled my old gray suit out of mothballs, I came to the conclusion its days were numbered. I picked out a new one a couple of days ago, but it needed some alterations."

"Can't wait to see it." She slipped off her coat, then tugged her wallet from the tote. "Be right back after I get some coffee."

Diana greeted her at the counter. "Haven't seen you since church on Sunday. Busy week?"

"Between chamber business and this Christmas project, I hardly have a spare minute." Brooke eyed the pastries in the display case. "Could I have a blueberry muffin and a mocha latte?"

"Coming right up." Filling a ceramic mug at the espresso machine, Diana glanced over her shoulder with a wink. "Another coffee date with our handsome Pastor O'Grady. Cool!"

"Stop it, will you? We're just taking care of some committee business."

"Mmm-hmm." Diana set the coffee and muffin on the counter. "Which totally explains why he invited you to be his date for his sister's wedding."

Brooke's mouth flattened. "Dad must have ratted me out."

"This is small-town Juniper Bluff, remember? Nobody's business is strictly their own."

"So I'm learning. And for the record, it isn't a *date*-date. He just invited me as a friend." Her unopened wallet tucked firmly beneath her arm, she picked up her order and offered a sugary-sweet smile. "I'd almost forgotten you still owe me unlimited coffee on the house."

"All right, but I reserve the right to cancel said agreement at the first indication of raised voices."

Brooke had no intention of letting it come to that—not because she didn't want to pay for her coffee, but because she sincerely hoped her petty bickering with Shaun was in the past. She liked him. A lot. And there was no question they were good together—in a collaborative, get-things-done kind of way, of course.

Of course.

Returning to the table, she strove to subdue the tumble of emotions plaguing her in the weeks since she'd returned to Texas. It wasn't like her to feel so out of control, and she couldn't let it continue.

She set down her mug with such force that coffee sloshed over the rim. "Oh, no."

Shaun half stood and began mopping up the spill with one of his napkins. "Everything okay? You look a little rattled."

"A permanent state of being these days." Making sure no drips had landed on her chair, she carefully sat down.

He paused a beat too long. "If the Christmas project is causing too much pressure, you can always let me carry more of the load."

Raising her eyes to his, she saw no condemnation or resentment there, only concern. "I just need to get through the holidays, and staying busy is the only thing that's helping."

With a nod of understanding, he took a ballpoint pen from his pocket and flipped open his steno pad. "Okay, so what should our priorities for tomorrow be?"

"The playground still needs attention." Brooke consulted her tablet computer. "And Emily may be bringing out some landscaping plants. But first, what's the status of the broken washers?"

"Kent went out yesterday afternoon with the parts he'd ordered. Everything's up and running now."

"Wonderful." Nibbling on her muffin, she blocked out everything else and focused all her attention on the details of the project.

An hour later, they'd agreed upon four main goals for tomorrow's workday. Number one was to spruce up the playground and repair any broken equipment. Number two, the landscaping. Number three, committee members would go door-to-door asking each resident about needs or problems specific to their home and then begin addressing those to the extent possible. And the final goal was to send a couple of artistically skilled volunteers to repaint the entrance sign at the road.

Brooke drained the last drop from her mug. She'd switched to plain decaf after finishing her mocha and had long ago lost count of how many times Diana had stopped by with refills—whether only as a solicitous server or secretly spying on them, Brooke wouldn't hazard a guess. Probably both.

"Well, we did it." She flipped the cover closed on her tablet. "And, amazingly, without a single argument."

Shaun grinned. "See? All things are possible with God."

She attempted a laugh, but it fell flat. His words were an uncomfortable reminder that he was much more in step with the Lord than she was. Hands clasped beneath her chin, she asked, "How do you do it?"

"Do what?"

"Put all your trust in God. Even when it feels like He isn't answering."

Shaun tucked his pen into his shirt pocket, then released a slow, thoughtful breath. "I do it because I don't know any other way to live. Because living outside God's will is not a wise place to be."

"But how do you *know* whether you're in God's will? How do you know if you're making the right choices?"

He reached across the table to take her hand. "Where's this coming from, Brooke?"

The coffee-break crowd was thinning, and behind her, Diana bustled about clearing tables. This wasn't a conversation she needed her sister-in-law to overhear. "Never mind. I should get back to the office."

By the time she'd gathered up her things and started for the door, Shaun caught up and walked her out. He drew her to a halt several steps down the sidewalk. "Unless you really do have something pressing at work, I think you'd be better served talking this out."

"I'm sure it's just my new-kid-in-town adjustment period." She heaved an exaggerated shrug. "That's normal, right? I'll be fine." Whirling around she stepped off into the street.

Tires screeched. A horn blasted. Her tote crashing to the ground, she stared into the grill of a big blue pickup that had braked only inches away.

"Brooke!" Shaun appeared instantly at her side, his strong arms supporting her as he guided her back to the sidewalk. His gaze swept her from head to toe before he pulled her against his chest and held on tight. "Thank God you're okay!"

Trembling, she squeezed her eyes shut, her face buried in his shoulder. "I'm such an idiot."

Someone tapped her on the shoulder. The face of the pickup driver loomed close, concern furrowing his brow. "I'm so sorry, ma'am! Are you sure you're okay?"

"Yes, I'm fine." The shakes were beginning to diminish, and now she felt foolish to still be wrapped in Shaun's arms. She stiffened and pulled away. "It was totally my fault for not checking traffic."

Nodding uncertainly, the driver handed her her tote. "You dropped this. Hope nothing's broken."

Oh, great. Her tablet. She was almost afraid to look.

Even worse, a crowd had gathered. A few had their cell phones out, probably videoing her stupidity.

Diana pushed through. "Brooke! What on earth happened? Are you okay?"

"For the millionth time, yes! Everybody can officially quit fussing over me." She gave her jacket hem a tug. "I am now going to step carefully off the curb, cross the street after looking both ways and then make my way to the chamber of commerce. Ta-ta, all!"

Going straight back to work was the *last* thing Brooke needed after a scare like that, and Shaun had no intention of allowing her to do so. He hooked an arm around her waist. "No arguments. I'm escorting you directly to that gazebo over there, and we're going to sit quietly until your breathing and heart rate return to normal."

She released a tremulous chuckle. "Now look who's getting all bossy and take-charge."

"I have my moments." Reaching the square, he made a right turn on the path leading to the gazebo. She might claim she was fine, but with his arm pressed against her rib cage, he could feel every quivering inhalation.

As they climbed the steps, a mother with two small children started down. "We saw what happened," the woman said. She withdrew an unopened bottle of water from a small picnic cooler and handed it to Brooke. "Maybe this will help. Glad you weren't hurt."

With a tight smile, Brooke murmured her thanks, then set her hand on the taller child's shoulder. "Let my mistake be a lesson, kids. Always look both ways when you cross the street, and always hold your mom's—" her voice broke "—hand."

Giving the woman a polite nod, Shaun guided Brooke to one of the benches inside the gazebo. He took off his own jacket and tucked it around her, then pulled her beneath his arm. She resisted for only a moment before relaxing against his side. He let her rest there for a few minutes as they watched the citizens of Juniper Bluff go about their normal routine.

There was plenty to like about this town, he decided—

friendly people who cared enough to stop whatever they were doing to offer an encouraging word or lend a hand. If he weren't headed back to the mission field, he wouldn't mind settling here. Especially if Brooke—

He hit the brakes on that train of thought before it could leave the station.

"Thank you," she whispered, straightening. Her breathing seemed steadier now. She uncapped the water bottle and took a few sips. "Did I mention I feel utterly ridiculous?"

"Nearly getting mowed down by a two-ton behemoth is enough to shake up the hardiest soul."

She cast him a sidelong glance, the sparkle in her eyes reassuring him. "Is that really how much a pickup truck weighs?"

"I have no idea. But it sounded authoritative, didn't it?" He adjusted his jacket higher on her shoulders. "Anyway, you've given the volunteers plenty they can gossip about tomorrow. If it's anything like the proverbial fish story, by then the truck will be the size of a Sherman tank."

"That's me, Brooke Willoughby, chronic overachiever."

He had a suspicion there was more truth than humor in her choice of words. And he decided they were a lot more alike than he'd first wanted to admit—but with one crucial difference. His idealism led him to strive for the very best in his attempts to follow God's will. Brooke seemed driven by an innate need to control her own life. Maybe they both needed to strike a balance.

"I'm going to ask you a pointed question," he said, shifting to face her. "And whatever you answer, I hope you'll be honest with yourself if not with me."

She looked up with a dubious frown. "Okay... I guess."

"How's your prayer life these days?"

Her brown-eyed gaze sharpened briefly before she glanced away. She studied the label on the water bottle as if looking for her answer there. "It's been better," she admitted with a sigh. "Guess I haven't believed for a while that God's listening."

"Have you tried pausing your breakneck pace long enough to be sure you're listening to Him?"

Her whole body sagged forward. "I'm not sure I'd even recognize God's voice anymore."

Boy, did he know that feeling! How could he presume to help Brooke find her faith footing when lately he'd struggled so much with his own? It had been two weeks now since his last talk with Henry Voss, and each day since, he'd been intending to call and accept the position in Jordan. But every time he'd picked up the phone, something had stopped him. Henry would be calling back in the next day or so expecting a final decision, and then there'd be no more putting it off.

"My missions director wants me back in Jordan." The statement came out before he even knew he was going to tell her.

She straightened. Was that a flicker of disappointment in her eyes? "Are you going?"

"Probably. God hasn't told me no."

"Do you... I mean how do you really know if God's saying yes or no to something?" Honest curiosity filled her tone. "Or maybe directing you to something entirely different?"

"Good question. For me, it's a gut feeling I can't reason away. Or sometimes a passage from Scripture seems to leap off the page at me, as if God knew it was exactly what I needed right then. One thing I've learned, though," he said, hands clasped between his knees, "if I'm not spending time in prayer and the Word, I'm a whole lot less likely to discern God's direction."

Brooke nodded thoughtfully. "I need to be doing more of that, myself." With a deep inhalation, she stood and faced him with a smile. "I really do need to get back to work now. Thank you for…" Her helpless shrug spoke more than words. "For everything. But most of all, for being you."

Warmth spread across his chest, and those neon detour signs flashed brighter than ever in his mind. *What are You trying to tell me, Lord?* Because as close as these past several days had brought them, any kind of a lasting future with Brooke seemed, if not impossible, then too implausible to hope for.

Chapter Eleven

Shaun was right—Brooke needed to work a little harder on her relationship with the Lord. If it took nearly getting hit by a truck to be her wakeup call, maybe it was about time she got down to business. A different kind of business than was typical for her, but far more urgent.

And his announcement about accepting a call to Jordan? She'd known all along he planned to return to the mission field, so why had the news hit her so hard?

Because maybe you're developing feelings for the guy?

This was most certainly something to pray about.

On Saturday morning, upon first seeing him at the mobile home park, she endured a discomfiting moment. Then he smiled, and something deep beneath her heart surged upward, making it hard to breathe. She felt her lips spreading into a welcoming smile of her own as she murmured a breathy "Hi."

"Hi, yourself." He ambled over from the playground. "How are you today?"

"Fine. A good night's sleep can do wonders." Or would have if she'd actually managed it. She'd sat up in bed until well past midnight with her Bible open in her lap to the Psalms. Mom had found so much comfort there during her illness, often asking Dad or Brooke to read her favorite passages aloud, so it seemed only right that Brooke should return to those verses as she found her own way back to God.

"A couple of us got here early, so we started on the playground equipment," Shaun said.

"Ever the early bird." She rolled her eyes in a pretense of sarcasm, when secretly his promptness had become one of the qualities she appreciated about the man. "As soon as a few more arrive, we'll start visiting with the tenants about anything specific they might need done."

By shortly after nine o'clock, they had a full contingent of volunteers on hand, and they clocked through the day's tasks one by one. As jobs were completed and people began to head home, Brooke and Shaun stood with Mr. Zamora near the road as he admired the newly painted Whitetail Valley Mobile Home Park entrance sign.

"I cannot believe how much you have done in only two weekends," the man said, shaking each of their hands in turn. "You have truly given our residents a place to enjoy and take pride in."

"We're not through yet," Brooke said. "We'll be back the first weekend of December to take care of any last-minute items, and we also have the Christmas shop coming up. Lots of donations have already come in."

Mr. Zamora's eyes shone with gratitude. "Everyone is already getting excited about the shop. For many, you are making this their best Christmas ever."

A lump formed in Brooke's throat. It might not be *her* best Christmas ever, but somehow, knowing she'd made a difference in the lives of these families, that was okay. And wasn't making a long-term difference exactly what Shaun had insisted upon from the start? Why in the world had they argued about it so hard and long?

After they'd said goodbye to Mr. Zamora, Shaun walked with her to her car. "Feel like celebrating a job well done with dinner at Casa Luis?"

"I could go for some cheesy enchiladas."

"Great. I'll follow you over."

Dinner in a corner booth, with nothing more pressing on her mind than making sure she didn't spoil her appetite for the entrée by eating too many chips and salsa, was the most relaxed Brooke had felt in too long to remember. It might be merely exhaustion after a long and productive day…or it might be the company. If she weren't entertaining thoughts of accepting Zach's offer to come back to work for him in LA, or if Shaun weren't making plans to leave for Jordan after the holidays, who knew what might have developed from their chance friendship?

She sipped her iced tea. "How does this missionary thing work? Do you get to come back for holidays and such with your family?"

"Not as often as I'd like. But when you're serving overseas, the friendships you make become a different kind of family, where everybody's in the same situation and we're all doing our best to buoy each other's spirits."

"Still, it seems kind of sad." The bite of enchilada she was about to take suddenly didn't look so appetizing. She laid aside her fork.

Shaun extended his hand across the table. "Missing your mom?"

She nodded. "I know I shouldn't be dreading Thanksgiving and Christmas so much, but the thought of her not being there…" Her fingers found his, and she welcomed the comforting touch. "What makes it even harder is that my dad seems to be dealing with Mom's loss so much better than I am. He's even found a new lady friend at church."

"Is it serious?"

"He says they're just friends." She exhaled a heavy breath. "But the thought of anyone taking Mom's place—"

"You've got to believe he isn't seeing it that way."

"I know. Which is why I get so mad at myself for feeling the way I do." Picking up her fork again, she poked at the mound of refried beans. "But I'm going to work harder on this prayer thing. Last night I started reading my mother's favorite psalms."

Shaun smiled his approval. "I often start my prayer time with a psalm. It's never hard to find one that speaks directly to what I'm going through."

"Do you ever find answers to your prayers there?"

"Sometimes." His mouth flattened as he looked toward the growing dusk beyond the window. "Sometimes not."

Seeing the turmoil in his expression brought a twinge of guilt. As understanding as he'd been of her issues, maybe he could use the same empathetic support from her. "What answers are you hoping for, Shaun? Is this about your decision to go to Jordan?"

Jaw firm, he met her gaze. "The decision's made. I spoke with my director last night. I'll be leaving the first week of January."

His words forced her back against the seat. "You've known all day and you didn't say anything?"

"We needed to stay focused on today's task list." He offered a weak smile. "Telling you privately is one reason I asked if we could have dinner together."

"Yes, but we've been here nearly an hour, and this is the first time you've brought it up." Her throat clenched.

She didn't know whether these feelings were anger or sadness—or both. "As of yesterday morning, you still sounded uncertain. It sounds like God finally gave you your answer."

Did a nonanswer count? Because that was what it felt like to Shaun. Before he'd made the call to Henry last night, he'd asked God straight out for clear direction, even going as far as trying a technique he considered little more than superstition—letting the Bible fall open on its own, blindly setting his finger on the page and taking that verse as the Lord's final word on the current prayer issue.

So of course, his finger landed in the book of Jeremiah: *The heart is deceitful above all things.*

How could he claim his growing feelings for Brooke as God's doing and not merely the workings of his sinful human heart? Those detour signs he'd been imagining were the result of his own doubts and confusion. He had no business attributing them to God.

And yet, looking across the table at Brooke, reading the hurt and disappointment in her eyes, he couldn't help but wonder what might have been.

She crumpled her napkin beside her half-eaten meal, then swiveled to signal their server. "Check, please?"

"Let me." Shaun had intended to buy her dinner anyway. Now, it was the least he could do.

"Thanks, but I prefer to pay my own way." The coldness in her tone cut right through him.

Stopping beside their table, the server flipped through his order pad. "Y'all wanted separate checks?"

"No," Shaun said.

"Yes." Brooke spoke over him.

"This is my treat." He managed to smile at the server while also casting Brooke a pointed glare.

"Shaun—"

He snatched the ticket out of the server's hand. "Thank you. The food was great."

Shooting daggers at Shaun, Brooke grabbed her purse and jacket as she scooted out of the booth. In his race to toss some bills on the table and catch up before she made it to her car, he nearly upended a waiter's serving tray laden with four platters of steaming fajitas and all the fixings. She reached the door two steps ahead of him and shoved past a family just on their way in. Edging around them out the door, Shaun offered his apologies.

"Brooke, will you wait up, please?" He caught her by the elbow as she crossed the parking lot. "I'm sorry. I never thought my decision would upset you so much."

She swiped at wetness on her cheeks while choking out a laugh. "I'm totally overreacting. Ignore me, okay?"

"No. I need to understand what's going on here."

"What's going on is I'm an emotional basket case over the coming holidays, and all kinds of things are hitting me wrong." Flicking a golden brown curl off her shoulder, she turned to him with the phoniest smile he'd ever seen. "I'm happy for you, Shaun. Really."

He wanted to believe her, and missing her mother this time of year certainly could account for her up-and-down moods. So why did he have the feeling there was more to it? He'd like to shelter her in his arms as he had yesterday at the gazebo, but he wasn't getting those kinds of vibes from her tonight. Probably not a good idea anyway, because the thought of holding her again stirred longings he couldn't afford to give in to, not with the Jordan assignment looming.

"So, um…" She was fumbling for her keys. "Thank you for dinner."

Gathering his senses, he held her door as she climbed in behind the wheel. "You're welcome. See you in church tomorrow?"

A tight smile was her only reply. Moments later, her little red car sped out of the parking lot.

When Shaun didn't see Brooke in church the next morning, he worried even more. He spotted her father, though, seated between Tripp and Diana on one side and a silver-haired woman on the other. Must be the lady friend Brooke had seemed so bothered by. After worship ended, Shaun debated about asking Mr. Willoughby if Brooke was okay, but before he had the chance, Emily Ingram snagged him.

"I simply can't express how delighted I am with how you and Brooke have spearheaded our Christmas outreach this year," she gushed. "This is possibly the committee's best service project ever."

"Thanks. It's a team effort for sure." From the corner of his eye, Shaun glimpsed the Willoughby family on their way out. Guess he'd have to wait to ask about Brooke. "Just a few things to wrap up at the mobile home park and then get the Christmas store organized."

"Alma's outdone herself getting donations. Those families are going to be so blessed."

"It's been a blessing to be of service to them."

Her brows dipped. "I fully appreciate the nature of your missionary calling, which I suppose means you won't be around to help plan next year's outreach?"

"No, ma'am. I was going to tell everyone at the meeting tomorrow night, but I'm headed to Jordan in January."

"Their gain, our loss. At least we'll have Brooke, though. She's quite the go-getter."

"She is that." No point in bursting Emily's bubble with talk of the possible departure of both her project organizers if Brooke did return to LA.

Kent came up beside him. "Erin's not gonna be happy if we're late for Sunday dinner. Ready to go?"

Grateful for an excuse to break away, Shaun told Emily he'd see her tomorrow night.

Sunday dinners with Erin, Avery and Kent had become a regular thing since he'd come to town, and it was always a treat to see what his sister had cooking. His older brother, Greg, had also arrived in town this weekend and planned to stay through the wedding next Saturday. No doubt they'd all be running around like crazy helping with last-minute wedding details.

Today provided a good opportunity for Shaun to tell his family about his decision. After a meal of Erin's savory pot roast followed by banana pudding for dessert, he sat forward and cleared his throat. "I have a bit of news to share. I've accepted an assignment to serve in Jordan beginning the first of the year."

Erin's mouth fell open. She didn't look happy. "You're really going? But I thought…"

"Yeah, little brother," Greg said with a frown. "Guess we all hoped this sabbatical meant you'd stay around for a while."

"I have to go where God sends me." Shaun stiffened. Did his reply sound as canned to his family as it suddenly did to his own ears? "I mean, this position is a perfect fit for me. And the need is real. How could I turn it down?"

No one said anything. Even his usually talkative

young niece sat mutely, arms locked across her tiny chest and her lower lip poking out.

He looked from one to the other in search of any sign of support or understanding. The closest he came was Kent's sympathetic half smile.

"I get where you're coming from," Kent began softly. "You feel called to serve, and that's an honorable thing. But I understand their feelings, too. My family wasn't real happy when I enlisted in the navy, and each time I deployed was harder on them than the last."

"This isn't like I'm heading into a war zone." Why did he feel like he had to defend his reasoning? "Jordan is a very safe country, and I'll be living in a nice section of Amman. Good internet service, too, so I'll never be out of touch."

Releasing a heavy sigh, Erin rose and came around the table. She draped her arms around his neck and kissed him on the cheek. "We don't mean to be downers for you. It's just that we've loved so much having you close by for a change." She sniffled. "It'll be awful having to say good-bye again."

His sister had no idea how hard it was for him each time he packed up and said goodbye to his family, knowing he might not see them again for months or years at a time, but he doubted that would be much consolation. "I'll miss all of you, too. We've got the next several weeks together, though, so let's make the most of them." Squeezing her hand, he winked up at her. "Including celebrating the marriage of a couple who's pretty special to me."

His remark seemed to lighten the mood all around. With good-natured banter, they all pitched in to clear the table and put away the leftovers. When Kent and Erin excused themselves afterward to review their wedding checklist, Greg suggested he and Shaun walk off some of their dinner. Anticipating Greg's ulterior motives, Shaun prepared himself for more of his brother's thoughts about the Jordan assignment.

They hadn't made it to the end of the block before Greg said, "Okay, little brother, some honesty here. I've seen you so enthusiastic about a call to serve overseas that you were chomping at the bit to get on the plane. I've also witnessed your nervous anticipation about going to a new place. But this is the first time I've sensed genuine doubt. What gives?"

Wow. He had no idea his brother could read him that well. Shoulders hunched against the chilly air, he tucked his hands deeper into his jacket pockets. "I admit I struggled with this decision. But it's as I said. I've got the right qualifications and nothing keeping me here."

"That isn't the way Erin sees it." Greg elbowed him. "I hear you've met someone."

He meant Brooke, obviously. "I've known her all of one month. Which is long enough to determine neither of us is ready for anything more." *Liar, liar, pants on fire.* They both might claim they weren't ready, but there was definitely something *more* between them.

"Just sayin'." Greg paused at the next corner. "We miss you when you're overseas, but we'd all feel a lot more at ease about it if we knew you weren't alone over there. If you had a life partner to share in your ministry."

It wasn't as if Shaun hadn't longed for the same thing for himself. But Brooke? He could never see her being happy anywhere but big-city USA.

Brooke had no good reason for skipping church Sunday morning. Except one. She didn't feel like running into Shaun.

Well, two reasons, actually. She didn't feel like seeing her dad acting chummy with Lydia, either.

So over breakfast she'd told him that after spending all day yesterday at the mobile home park, she had a headache and needed to catch up on her rest. Since Dad had worked as hard as she had, her excuse was flimsy at best, but he accepted it without question.

It seemed so wrong that she should finally meet a man who inspired her and challenged her and—yes—made her heart beat faster, only to realize there was no chance they could ever be together.

But why couldn't you go with him? How daunting could living overseas be?

For one thing, she couldn't bear being quite *that* far from her family. Besides, Tripp and Diana might decide to start their own family soon, and wouldn't it be fun to spoil a precious niece or nephew? Living back in LA might mean a few hours on a plane whenever she wanted to visit, but that was nothing compared to the cost and discomfort of a transatlantic flight!

Face it, Brooke. You're a pampered middle-class American who wouldn't know the first thing about being a missionary's wife.

And she couldn't believe she was even thinking along those lines! She and Shaun were friends. Period.

The church seniors group had planned a Sunday afternoon excursion to go antiquing in Fredericksburg, which Dad had signed up for—Lydia, too, most likely—so Brooke had the house to herself. With her laptop open on the kitchen table, she started a pot of coffee and then set to work on some chamber business. Wouldn't hurt to get a head start preparing for the various meetings coming up this week. Not caring to be lectured about working on the Sabbath, she made sure her computer was safely stowed in her room well before Dad arrived home from Fredericksburg.

Whistling a jaunty tune, he breezed in a few minutes past six. Brooke had just taken some leftovers out of the fridge to heat up for a light supper. "Somebody's in a happy mood."

"It was a fun day." He tossed his jacket on a hook by the back door. "Don't worry about anything for me. Just had a grilled cheese and malt at the drugstore soda fountain."

The smile he couldn't seem to keep off his face suggested he hadn't dined alone. Swallowing a catty remark, Brooke scooped a heaping spoonful of broccoli chicken casserole onto a plate and set it in the microwave.

As if reading her mind, Dad came up beside her and placed an arm around her waist. "Lydia and I are just friends, honey. Her husband passed away three years ago, and it's been good for both of us to have someone who understands what it's like to lose a spouse."

"I'm sorry, Dad." She rested her temple against his. "If spending time with Lydia makes you happy, that's all I care about." All she had a *right* to care about.

The microwave beeped. Though she smiled for her father's sake as she carried her supper to the table, it occurred to her that maybe Dad's friendship with Lydia wasn't the real issue. Maybe it was the fact that everyone else in her life seemed to be finding their way after Mom's death, while she'd only managed to keep running in place.

Chapter Twelve

The Monday evening committee meeting ran smoothly. Shaun began with a recap of the two workdays at the mobile home park and enumerated the tasks still remaining. "One more Saturday should do it," he said. "However, we won't have Kent's handyman skills to count on, since he and my sister will be somewhere warm and sunny enjoying their honeymoon."

A chorus of "oohs" filled the room, and Kent's face reddened.

Emily reached across the table to pat his arm. "We're all so happy for you and Erin. You make such a cute couple, and that precious little Avery will be blessed to have you as her new daddy."

"Thanks." He ducked his head. "Count on us to help with the Christmas store, though. Erin said she'd bake some cookies for the refreshment table. Oh, and Alma, she said to tell you she'll donate a couple of her one-of-a-kind baskets."

"Speaking of the Christmas store…" Brooke took over the discussion as they hammered out the details for organizing the donations, issuing vouchers to the mobile home park families, then setup and staffing.

Her professionalism never failed to impress Shaun—and it wasn't just her organizational skills or her proficiency with computers. She could get to the heart of the matter quickly, and she had a way of dealing with people that made them feel respected and appreciated.

True, not always so much with him, considering their volatile history. But most of their disagreements could be blamed on his own stubborn streak. Sitting back to watch her run this portion of the meeting, he kept wishing they'd met under different circumstances. If he weren't committed to missionary service, if she weren't so married to her career...

But then they wouldn't be the same people. And if either one of them were different, would the spark of attraction have been nearly as powerful?

"Shaun, did you hear me?" She was looking straight at him, her brow furrowed and a funny half smile curling her lips.

He fumbled with his steno pad. "Sorry, I was reviewing my notes. What did you say?"

"I asked if you have anything to add before we turn the meeting back over to Emily."

"Uh, no, I'm good."

Emily concluded with a quick rundown of everything they'd covered. "We'll meet again two weeks from tonight, at which time we'll evaluate our progress and finalize plans for the Christmas store. Everyone have a lovely Thanksgiving, and I'll see many of you at Kent and Erin's wedding festivities this Saturday."

Shaun stepped closer as Brooke gathered up her things. "How are your Thanksgiving plans coming along?" His tone softened with concern. "Are you doing okay?"

She shrugged. "Did I tell you we're all having dinner at the assisted living center with Diana's great-aunt?"

"Right, and then the therapy pets are visiting. Should be fun." He followed her into the corridor as Emily switched off lights behind them.

"I might have to adopt a dog of my own one of these days. I know Dad wouldn't mind having one around, especially now..." Her mouth firmed, and she walked a little faster.

He lengthened his stride to keep up. "I'm a dog lover, too—we always had pets when I was growing up." And why, suddenly, did he have the urge to rush out and adopt the first stray that came along?

Exiting the building, Brooke paused. "I'd love it if you could stop by the center while the therapy pets are there. Diana says the residents light up every time the pets visit."

Shaun felt like he might be lighting up right now, and only a tiny part of it was due to the idea of watching senior citizens having fun with the animals. "What time?"

"Dinner's at one o'clock, so I think Diana's planning on around two thirty."

"That might work. Our family's having Thanksgiving dinner at Kent's. His parents are driving down that same day, so we won't eat before five."

"Perfect." Tossing a jaunty smile over her shoulder, Brooke continued toward her car. "You can help me with Ginger, Diana's corgi. That little critter's a handful!"

"I'll look forward to it." Shaun waved as he climbed into his rusty green hatchback. Someday he'd have to replace this old thing. Maybe a spiffy newer-model SUV, or even a small pickup—

Where are you going with this, O'Grady? First a dog,

then a truck? Next thing, what—his own brick ranch-style house on prime Hill Country acreage? Those kinds of things went along with stability, a wife and kids, the Great American Dream. Nothing wrong with any of those things, per se, but it wasn't the life Shaun had chosen for himself. He was committed to serving God on the mission field, and he wasn't about to bail on the Lord now. Come January, he'd be on a plane to Amman and on to the next phase of his missionary career.

As for the pinch in his gut every time he thought about leaving for Jordan…nothing more than nervousness about heading into a new situation. That was his story, and he was sticking to it.

Inviting Shaun to the assisted living center on Thanksgiving afternoon probably hadn't been the best idea Brooke had ever had. What was the point of spending even more time with a guy who would be out of her life by year's end? Even so, anticipation built as the day drew near. Good thing she had plenty at the chamber to keep her mind occupied.

Returning to the office with Inez after the Wednesday noon Lions Club meeting, she felt pleasantly stuffed after a pre-Thanksgiving luncheon that included ham, candied sweet potatoes and a huge slice of pecan pie. "I need to run five miles if I want to eat again tomorrow."

"Tell me about it," her boss said with a groan. She motioned Brooke into her office. "Sit down a minute. I need to share something."

Brooke's first thought was a silent *uh-oh*. Her face must have shown it, because Inez quickly waved a hand.

"It's all good, Brooke. I just thought you should hear some of the feedback I'm getting from our chamber members." Steepling her fingertips, Inez smiled warmly. "I was sitting between Alan Glazer and the mayor at lunch, and both were extremely complimentary of the work you're doing here. And they aren't the only ones. I've been hearing good things about you ever since we brought you on board."

"Thank you." A bubble of pride swelled beneath Brooke's heart.

"You'll recall during your initial interview that I expressed a few reservations about how your big-city work ethic would translate to a small-town chamber of commerce. But after seeing you in action this past month, I believe you're exactly what Juniper Bluff needs."

Brooke drew a quick breath. "To be honest, I've had my reservations, too. I can be a little too enthusiastic at times, especially when I start pushing new ways of doing things."

"Sometimes pushing is a good thing—" Inez chuckled "—especially when certain mindsets are resistant to progressive change. What I'm trying to say," she continued, leaning closer, "is that I hope you're as happy in your job here as we are to have you."

Inez's words touched her in ways she couldn't describe. "I have another confession to make." Eyes lowered, she continued, "Several days ago, I had a call from my former boss at the advertising firm. He said he'd always have a position for me if I ever wanted to come back…and I was almost ready to accept."

Lips pressed together, Inez inched backward. "I'd hate to think you'd leave us in the lurch like that, and after so short a time."

"I wouldn't," Brooke rushed to say. "It's true I've questioned whether Juniper Bluff is where I need to be right now, but mostly for personal reasons, not because I haven't felt fulfilled in my work here." Her shoulders sagged. "It's…it's been a difficult year."

Inez's expression turned sympathetic. "Need to talk about it?"

For the next hour, Brooke tearfully poured out her ongoing struggles with grief, worry, doubt and confusion. Inez interrupted once to make them each a cup of herbal tea and replace the box of tissues Brooke had emptied. Good thing there wasn't much happening at the chamber on Thanksgiving Eve, because for Brooke to pull herself together would have required a major act of will, not to mention completely redoing her makeup.

As her words ran down, she uttered a weak laugh. "Guess I really did need to talk."

Now seated in the visitor's chair next to Brooke, Inez leaned over to offer a hug. "Do you think you could stand some advice from a *slightly* older and wiser friend?"

With a teary-eyed smile, Brooke nodded.

"First of all, every single thing you're feeling is perfectly normal after the loss of a loved one."

"So I'm not going crazy?"

"Not so far." Inez winked. "Second, you need to invest more time and energy taking care of yourself. Your father and your brother are grown men, and it sounds like they're managing their own lives just fine."

"They've been trying to tell me the same thing. And you're right. By channeling all my attention toward family and work, I've short-circuited my own grieving process."

Snapping her fingers, Inez adopted a phony British accent to say, "By George, I think she's got it!"

Brooke sank deeper into her chair. "The question is, what do I do with it?"

"Well, that's easy…and hard. What you *don't* do is rush into any ill-considered decisions." Inez cast her a stern glance. "Like jumping on the next plane to LA."

"Don't worry, that's officially off the table. If anything's become clearer today, it's that I belong right here in Juniper Bluff."

"Good." Consulting her watch, Inez stood and tugged Brooke to her feet. "Now, go shut down your computer and get out of here. I don't want to see you again until Monday morning—except at church, of course. Spend these next few days enjoying your family and enjoying life."

"I'll try."

"Oh, and before you go, here's one more *don't*."

Thoughts already spinning with her boss's sage advice, Brooke couldn't imagine Inez had left anything out. "I'm listening."

"Don't close your heart to love. There's something special going on between you and Shaun, so give it a chance. Yes, I know he's called to missionary service," she hurried on before Brooke could protest, "but if what you two have is true love, God will work out the details."

There was no arguing against the power of God, that much Brooke could admit. And if these crazy stirrings in her heart meant she really was falling in love with Shaun…the Lord definitely had His work cut out for Him.

Shortly after ten o'clock on Thanksgiving Day, Erin and Avery arrived at Kent's with a carload of food. Shaun and Kent both hurried out to help her carry everything to the kitchen.

Hefting a huge roasting pan from the trunk, Shaun

nearly stumbled. "How many exactly are we expecting for dinner? Because this feels like about fifty pounds of turkey."

Avery reached around him for a much smaller container. "There's Mommy and Kent and you and Uncle Greg and my cousin Taylor and Kent's mommy and daddy. Oh, and me! So that's…" She paused to count on her fingers. "Eight! And Mommy made four pies so we get half a pie each."

"She's been practicing her math, in case you were wondering," Erin said.

Just then, Greg's SUV pulled up behind Erin's car, and he and his daughter, Taylor, climbed out. Taylor rushed over and flung her arms around Shaun's neck. "Uncle Shaun, it's so good to see you again!"

"You, too, kiddo," he choked out. "I'd hug you back, but I've kinda got my hands full."

"Oh, sorry. Let me help." Flipping short blond bangs off her forehead, Taylor grabbed one of the handles of the roasting pan. "Whoa, what's in here—a fifty-pound turkey?"

Shaun glared at Erin. "I rest my case."

"Wimps." Erin started toward the house with a stack of pie containers. "Keep up the complaining and there'll be no dessert for you."

It took three trips to get all the food inside, and the friendly banter never stopped. Shaun tried to remember the last time he'd spent the holidays with his family and decided it had been too long. He kept reminding himself he was storing up cherished Thanksgiving and Christmas memories this year—memories he could cling to during his time overseas. True, nothing compared to the real thing, but the Lord always managed to connect him with other faithful servants to become his surrogate family.

With everyone pitching in, Erin soon had a food prep assembly line going. Once the turkey was stuffed and in the oven, she sliced whole wheat baguettes to go along with the butternut squash soup she'd brought for lunch.

"This is amazing, sis." Shaun ladled a second helping of soup into his bowl. "How you managed to plan and prepare an entire Thanksgiving menu on top of last-minute wedding details, I will never know."

"Just doing what I love, for the people I love." She linked her arm through Kent's, and they shared a quick kiss.

Watching them brought a pinch to Shaun's gut. Until these last few weeks—more to the point, until he'd begun spending so much time with Brooke—he'd given little thought to what he'd been missing for so long. Lately, every time Brooke came to mind, the idea of leaving Juniper Bluff seemed less and less appealing.

On the other hand, staying made no sense, either. Besides the possibility that Brooke could be moving on soon, what opportunities were there in a small town like this for an unemployed missionary pastor? No, he'd committed to the Jordan assignment, and there'd be no backing out.

But first, he had another memory to make this afternoon, and a check of the time told him he'd better get over to the assisted living center. Promising Erin he'd be back in plenty of time to help get dinner to the table, he grabbed a jacket and hurried out.

Arriving at the center, he parked next to a red extended-cab pickup that had just pulled in. He recognized Kent's friend Seth Austin and his wife, Christina.

Seth opened the rear door, and a furry golden retriever wearing a blue service dog vest hopped to the ground. Tail wagging, the dog nosed up to Shaun.

"Looks like Gracie's made a new friend," Seth said with a laugh. "How's it going, Shaun? All set for a wedding on Saturday?"

"Erin and Kent are the ones with the most to do." Something in the dog's soft brown eyes drew him to his knees, and he knelt to scratch her behind the ears. "You're some special girl, you know that?"

"Oh, she knows, all right." Christina cast her husband a meaningful glance as she adjusted Gracie's vest.

Wondering what their shared look could mean, Shaun stood. "Is Gracie one of the therapy pets?"

"Yes, we joined the group a few months ago," Christina replied. "It's always interesting to see who Gracie's drawn to each time we visit. She seems to have a sixth sense about who needs her most."

Giving a thoughtful nod, Shaun walked with them to the entrance. Several other pet owners had already gathered in the lobby, and Shaun scanned the faces in search of Brooke. He spotted her on the opposite side of the room as she tried to calm a hyperactive corgi.

"Ginger, sit," she commanded, although without much force. "We can't go in to see everybody until Diana says they're ready."

Shaun excused himself to the Austins and strode over. "Need a little help?"

"Please! This little girl's about to make me crazy." She thrust the leash at Shaun.

He dropped to one knee and snapped the fingers of one hand while giving the leash a gentle tug with the other. "Sit."

The dog sat, a perky doggy grin lighting her face and her round eyes fixed on him.

"Got any treats?" Shaun murmured.

Brooke slipped him a handful from the baggie she produced. Ginger sat obediently as he offered her one.

"I'm officially impressed," Brooke said. "You're keeping the leash when we go in to see the residents."

Shaun wouldn't admit he was as surprised as Brooke at how well the dog was responding to him. Kent's hairy old mutt sure didn't give him this much respect. Of course, Skip didn't respect much of anything except suppertime and long naps in the easy chair.

Diana emerged from a set of double doors. "Okay, everyone, they're ready for us."

The procession of owners and pets filed into a large gathering room, where more than twenty elderly folks and their visiting family members waited with glowing faces. If Shaun hadn't had a firm grip on Ginger's leash, the dog would have ripped it from his hand in her excited rush toward a white-haired woman across the room.

"There's my Ginger-girl!" After accepting several wet doggy kisses, the woman looked up. "Thank you so much for bringing her, Brooke."

"Hi, Mrs. Stewart. It's great to see you again."

The woman clucked her tongue. "Aunt Jennie to you, dear. As Diana's best friend, you've always been like family. And who's this handsome young man with you?"

"This is my friend Shaun. He was helping me keep Ginger corralled in the lobby."

"I've been hearing all about your little dog," Shaun said. "She's obviously very special to you."

"Very special indeed." Mrs. Stewart returned to cuddling with her dog.

Diana strode over, a lop-eared rabbit cradled in her arms. "You can leave Ginger with Aunt Jennie. They'll be fine."

Brooke motioned toward two empty folding chairs in a quiet corner. "Want to get out of the fray?"

"Good idea." They maneuvered around wagging tails and beaming senior citizens. "This is an amazing ministry," Shaun said as they sat down. "And the pets are loving it, too."

"All Diana's doing. She had a dream and made it happen…with a little help from my veterinarian brother." Brooke tipped her head toward Tripp, where he and their dad sat with Jennie Stewart and Ginger. "Thank you again for coming. It means a lot."

Something in her tone caught Shaun's attention. He tilted his head to study her. "You okay?"

"I'm doing better." A pensive smile dimpled her cheeks. "Yep, definitely doing better."

"Can I ask what's changed?"

"For one thing, I'm praying more. Listening more, too. Yesterday my boss also gave me a lot to think about."

Hands clasped between his knees, he couldn't bring himself to look at her. "Anything you can share?"

"Some of it I'm still mulling over. But one thing she helped me realize is that I don't have the right or the power to control anyone else's happiness. I'm only responsible for my own."

"Sounds like good advice." Was this the part where she told him she'd soon be seeking happiness and fulfillment back in LA?

"So I think I'll be sticking around Juniper Bluff for the foreseeable future."

His head popped up. "You are?"

Her warm brown eyes held a look of contentment he hadn't seen there before. "Running back to my old job in LA wouldn't fix anything. It'd just be me trying to escape the messed-up parts of my life instead of embracing and learning from them."

"I'm happy for you, Brooke." He meant it, he really did. She deserved to be happy. She deserved every good thing God sent her way. So why did her decision to stay in Juniper Bluff feel like a knife through his heart? He wouldn't be around to miss her, anyway.

Not true. Wherever life took him, he'd miss this woman—miss what might have been—for the rest of his life.

Dusk was falling as Brooke, her father, Tripp and Diana said goodbye to Aunt Jennie and her neighbors at the center. Shaun had left an hour ago, needing to get back to Kent's in time for their family dinner.

It had been a good day, and Brooke had to admit the one-year anniversary of her mother's death hadn't been nearly as painful as she'd feared. Yes, there had been moments. More than once, she'd noticed Tripp struggling to keep a smile on his face. As hard as losing Mom had been for her, and even more so for Dad, her brother had carried a burden of guilt he should never have had to bear. His blood type would have made him a perfect match as Mom's kidney donor, but the Crohn's had made him ineligible. In the days leading up to Mom's funeral, he'd neglected his own health out of remorse, and they'd almost lost him, too.

So her family shouldn't wonder why she worried and fussed over them as she did. Hard as it would be, though, she truly intended to try cutting back. She only hoped they'd be patient with her and forgive her if she occasionally overstepped.

"Well, we did it." Diana stood on the sidewalk with her arm around Brooke while Tripp loaded Ginger and the rabbit crate into the back of their SUV.

"*You* did it," Brooke insisted. "I know I balked at first, but having dinner with your aunt and then bringing all the therapy pets for a visit was a wonderful idea. Mom would have loved every minute of it."

"She sure would have." Dad came up on Brooke's other side. He held a square foam container.

"What's in the box?"

He grinned. "Four slices of pumpkin pie I wheedled from the kitchen staff."

"Da-ad!" Brooke and Diana both chortled.

Watching the residents lavish affection on all the pets that afternoon, they'd laughed loud and often, and it felt good. It had also felt nice to share the day with Shaun. *If what you two have is true love, God will work out the details*, Inez had said. And if a future with him wasn't part of God's plan, she'd be grateful for the chance she'd been given to know him as a friend, and also because he'd helped her open her heart again to the possibilities of falling in love.

Chapter Thirteen

Less than a year ago, Brooke had been helping prepare for another wedding at Shepherd of the Hills, that time as Diana's maid of honor for a ceremony many had thought would never happen. For one reason, it had taken a long time for Diana to forgive Tripp for keeping his Crohn's disease a secret when he'd broken up with her ten years earlier. And for another, the twins Diana's very pregnant matron of honor, Christina Austin, was carrying at the time, chose that day to make their entrance into the world. The big church ceremony had been canceled, and later that afternoon the family and closest friends had reconvened for a more intimate wedding at the assisted living center so Diana's great-aunt could attend.

Brooke hoped Erin and Kent's wedding wouldn't turn out to be so dramatic. As one of the officiants, Shaun needed to be at the church early, so Brooke said she'd drive herself over. Since she didn't know either Kent or Erin that well yet, being a guest at their wedding felt a little awkward. Entering the foyer, she smiled at a few familiar faces before pausing to sign the guest book.

A side door opened, and a tiny voice called, "Brooke, over here."

She turned in surprise. "Erin?"

The petite redhead motioned her closer, inviting her into the white-carpeted bride's dressing room. "I'm so glad Shaun invited you. Once all this wedding folderol and the holidays are behind us, I'm hoping to get to know you much better."

Warmed by Erin's welcoming hug, Brooke swallowed over a sudden lump in her throat. "I hope so, too." She stepped back to admire Erin's lacy off-the-shoulder gown. "Wow, your dress is gorgeous!"

"Thank you! I'm not doing the veil this time. That seems to be the latest trend." Erin swiveled toward the mirror to tuck an already perfect auburn curl into place. "Not too much for a second-time-around bride, is it?"

"Absolutely not. You look stunning."

The door creaked open and Christina Austin slipped in with Erin's daughter, Avery, both wearing matching waltz-length forest-green dresses. "Got the twins all settled in the nursery, and Seth's grandparents are in charge of Joseph and Eva." Noticing Brooke, she cast her a mischievous grin. "And I promise, if anything happens to postpone this wedding—which I pray is *not* the case— it won't be my fault."

"Mine, either," Avery piped up, obviously clueless about the inside joke. "I've practiced and practiced to be the flower girl because I can't wait for Kent to be my new daddy!"

After some shared laughter, Brooke offered the bride her best wishes and then excused herself to find a seat in the sanctuary. Noticing Emily Ingram and her husband, she asked the usher if she could join them in their pew.

She'd barely sat down and said hello when Shaun strode over. He looked amazingly handsome in his new charcoal gray suit, white shirt and a tie in shades of green to match Christina's and Avery's dresses.

She rose and offered a shy smile. "Nice suit."

"Should be, considering what it cost me." Grinning, he ran a finger around the inside of his shirt collar. "I am so not used to dressing up this much."

"Well, considering the effect," she said, reaching up to straighten the knot of his tie, "you really ought to try it more often."

His voice grew husky. "Maybe I'll have to."

Behind her, Emily tittered, no doubt reading far more into the moment than she should. With a quiet *ahem*, Brooke lowered her tingling fingers to her sides. "I believe you have duties to attend to, Pastor O'Grady."

With a nod, he returned to the chancel, where Pastor Terry was making a last-minute microphone check at the lectern.

Emily touched shoulders with Brooke as she sat down. "Can't help but wonder if we'll be witnessing the marriage of another happy couple one day soon."

With feigned innocence, Brooke glanced around. "Anyone I know?"

Emily only chuckled. When the organist began the processional moments later, Brooke released a silent sigh of relief. She smiled as Erin's daughter led the way with a basket of long-stemmed red roses. Shaun's niece Taylor followed, met at the chancel by a young man the program listed as Elijah Bennet. Wanda Flynn, Erin's business partner at WE Design, came next, joining Ben Zipp, a gruff-looking white-haired man Emily said was Kent's boss from the hardware store. Christina followed, taking her husband Seth's arm as she neared the altar.

Then the music changed. Erin appeared at the church doors, escorted by her brother Greg, and Brooke could no longer keep herself from imagining what it would be like to marry the man of her dreams...a man who more and more resembled Shaun O'Grady. Yes, they were opposites in so many ways, but when they were in sync, something marvelous happened. If only he weren't determined to return to the mission field.

If only she weren't a dyed-in-the-wool spoiled middle-class American who spoke only one language and wouldn't know how to exist without a microwave oven, 200-channel cable TV and high-speed internet.

The service continued as Erin and Kent exchanged the special vows they'd written for each other. Pastor Terry gave a brief homily on the covenant of marriage. A soloist sang "The Lord's Prayer" as Erin and Kent knelt at the altar.

"And now receive this blessing," Shaun said, his right hand uplifted. "May the love of the Father guide you into true sacrificial love within the bonds of the new family God has created from this union. May you be each other's warmth and shelter, lover and friend." A catch in his voice made him pause. "And may you always bring out the best in each other as you grow in service to our Lord Jesus Christ, for we pray in His holy name. Amen."

Joyous music filled the sanctuary as the new Mr. and Mrs. Kent Ritter shared their first kiss as a married couple. Tears blurring her vision, Brooke rose with the other wedding guests and joined in the applause. Yes, she wanted this for herself someday, the Lord willing. Not merely the lovely gown and flowers and rapturous

music, but what came afterward—a lifetime to spend
with someone who looked at her the way Kent was looking at Erin.

The way Shaun was looking at her right this minute.

She tore her gaze away to watch the beaming couple
hurry down the aisle, little Avery between them looking
even more ecstatic than her mother, if that were possible. Seth and Christina followed arm in arm, their own
love evident in their sparkling eyes. And some interested
smiles certainly seemed to be passing between Wanda
Flynn and Ben Zipp.

Ushers directed the guests to a reception in the fellowship hall, where Brooke chatted with a few acquaintances. Tripp and Diana were among the guests, but she'd
just as soon steer clear of them in case they decided to
take a cue from Emily Ingram in the matchmaking de-
partment.

Shaun found her a few minutes later, tiny beads of
perspiration dotting his forehead. "Think anybody would
notice if I took this tie off now?"

"I certainly would." She cast him a sincere smile.
"Shaun, you looked so perfectly natural up there, totally in your element. It was a truly beautiful ceremony."

"Thanks. I'm glad I could do this for my sister." He
nodded toward the buffet table. "Shall we get something
to drink? I'm parched."

Before they'd taken two steps, Seth Austin rushed
over and snagged Shaun's elbow. "There you are. We're
all supposed to be in the sanctuary for photographs."

He grimaced. "Forgot all about it—or maybe I was
trying to."

"Guess you're stuck wearing your tie a while longer," Brooke said with a sympathetic frown. "I'll save

you some sweet tea." She snickered at his pinch-faced grimace.

Oh, Shaun, why'd you have to be so easy to fall for? She'd actually considered making excuses and slipping out early, before the romance cloud filling the air grew any thicker. Her velour bathrobe, fuzzy slippers and a steamy mug of hot cocoa might just be enough to chase away her always-the-wedding-guest-never-the-bride blues.

But she'd come as Shaun's plus-one, so it was only polite to wait for him. Once the wedding party made their appearance at the reception, she'd stay an acceptable half hour or so, congratulate the newlyweds, and then say her goodbyes.

Shaun's jaws ached from smiling so much. Would this photo shoot never end?

"Hang in there," Pastor Terry murmured as the photographer directed them into new positions. "This is all part of the job."

"Not the one *I* signed up for." Another camera flash made him wince. "No suits and ties involved with refugee work. And the last wedding ceremony I performed had to be at least six years ago, the first time I was serving in Jordan."

"So you're really going back, huh?"

"That's the plan."

The photographer peered out from behind the camera. "Pastor O'Grady, let's have a big smile, okay?"

He hadn't realized his smile had faltered.

A couple more flashes, and then, "Okay, pastors, all done with your part. Now, if we can have the bride's family…"

So not quite over for Shaun yet. He posed with Greg, Taylor, Erin, Avery and Kent for a few pictures, then more with Kent's parents added to the group, and finally the photographer packed up his gear to accompany the wedding party to the fellowship hall.

By then, most of the guests were enjoying catered barbecue and the sweet tea Shaun could barely get past his lips. He opted for ice water instead, then filled a plate with barbecue and sides. Glancing around, he spotted Brooke in one of their reserved seats at the family table, where she and Taylor had already struck up a conversation.

"Finally," he said, easing into the chair beside her. "Sorry it took so long."

"That's okay. Taylor was just telling me about her college equestrian team. You never told me your niece was such an accomplished rider."

"I, uh…guess I haven't kept up too well these past few years." This time he didn't hesitate to loosen his tie and shirt collar. Eager to change the subject, he spread a napkin in his lap. "How's the barbecue?"

Then he noticed Brooke had barely touched hers. "It's very good." She pushed coleslaw around with her fork. "But I probably shouldn't have filled up on appetizers."

He didn't have the same excuse for why his appetite had suddenly waned. With the day's adrenaline rush fading, he'd begun to sense the shaded differences in how he and Brooke were relating to each other. The good-natured gibes hadn't let up, but everything seemed less genuine, a pretense of how things used to be, before…

Before you realized you were falling in love with her.

The rest of the wedding party eventually made it through the gauntlet of well-wishers. After filling plates at the buffet, they took their places around the table. Shaun had never seen his sister look happier, and Avery looked like she was ready to burst.

"Are you ever going to tell us where you're going on your honeymoon?" Taylor asked.

Seth snorted. "Only thing they'll say is somewhere sunny and warm. And since I know they're driving and we've only been drafted to keep Avery for a week, I'm guessing Corpus Christi or Galveston."

Taylor rolled her eyes. "Bo-ring. Aunt Erin, you should have held out for Turks and Caicos or St. Lucia."

"Not everybody needs to travel somewhere far, far away to be hap—" Cutting herself off, Erin cast Shaun a look of apology. "I mean, there's no reason to go anywhere fancy since we'll be, um…" Her cheeks took on a rosy blush, and she looked to Kent for help.

All she got from him was a schoolboy grin.

When everyone had had time to enjoy the meal, Seth began a series of toasts honoring the bride and groom. Afterward, the DJ announced the first dance, and Erin and Kent took the floor, gazing into each other's eyes to the lyrics of "At Last." A few measures into the song, Greg invited a giggling Avery to the dance floor, and Seth and Christina soon followed.

Shaun turned to Brooke with a shy smile. "I'm not much of a dancer, but care to give it a try?"

"Oh, Shaun, I don't know if that's such a good idea."

He wasn't so sure, either, but how could he pass up what might be his last opportunity to hold this woman in his arms? Scooting his chair back, he reached for her hand. "Come on, you're my date for this affair, and I won't take no for an answer."

She hesitated briefly but allowed him to lead her to

the dance floor. Finding an open spot among the other couples, he tucked her right hand against his shoulder, his other hand resting at the small of her back. She smelled like cinnamon and citrus, and the brush of her hair against his cheek made him wish the music would never end.

It did, though, all too soon. She eased from his arms, her hands fluttering to her sides. "That was...nice."

"Yeah." When did his voice get so breathy?

The next song began with a pulsing beat that had everyone bouncing and jiving. Brooke shook her head. "Not my style."

"Mine, either." He escorted her back to their table, but when he pulled out her chair, she declined.

"Would anyone be offended if I slipped out?" she asked. "The busy week is catching up with me."

He swallowed his disappointment. "I'll walk you out to your car."

"No, stay and enjoy this time with your family." She tucked a silver clutch under her arm. "I'll give you a call early next week to go over the plans for our final workday at the park."

"Hard to believe we're almost to the home stretch." Maybe if he kept her talking, she wouldn't rush out.

It didn't work.

"Well, goodbye, Shaun, and thank you again for inviting me. The wedding was lovely. Please tell Erin and Kent how happy I am for them." Eyes bright—were those tears?—she hurried out.

The fast-tempo song ended, and Greg returned to the table. He was breathing much harder than his twenty-year-old daughter, still on the dance floor with Avery.

After a swig from his iced tea glass, Greg asked, "Did I just see your date leave?"

"Said she was tired." An excuse Shaun didn't totally buy. Sprawled in his chair, he loosened the knot of his tie a bit more, which only reminded him of Brooke's touch as she'd straightened it for him before the ceremony. Boy, he was a mess.

Greg came around the table to claim Brooke's empty chair. "You okay, bro?"

"Sure, I'm fine." *Not.* He was crushed. Confused. Questioning everything about the last few weeks, not to mention the whole rest of his life. *Why, God? Why would You let me fall for her and then send me to the other side of the world?*

Peering squint-eyed at him, Greg stroked his chin. "If I didn't know better, I'd think my little brother was in love."

"In love with a dream," he muttered. "We're too different. It could never work."

"I thought the same thing about Vivienne and me when we met in college. She was pure class, and I was a boring business major nerd." An incredulous smile spread across Greg's face as he looked toward the dance floor, where Taylor was showing Avery how to do the Floss. "I didn't know a thing about art or music, and she went cross-eyed when I talked about numbers. But somehow it worked. *We* worked. We made a beautiful daughter together, and we were crazy in love for all the years God gave us."

"I know you miss her," Shaun said. Regret swamped him again that he hadn't been able to make it home for Vivienne's funeral. Had it really been eight years already?

"What I'm trying to say is, don't let Brooke go just because it looks like everything's stacked against you. Things can change. People can change. You owe it to yourself—to each other—to give this relationship a chance."

Trudging in from the garage, Brooke tossed her clutch and coat onto a kitchen chair. "Dad, I'm home."

"Back already?" From his recliner in the den, her father glanced over from the football game he was watching. "Thought the festivities would still be going on."

"Oh, they are. Just not with me." She plopped onto the sofa with a groan.

Dad muted the TV. "What's wrong, honey? Are you coming down with something?"

Did a broken heart count? And how could she claim a broken heart when there'd never been any declarations of love?

The recliner footrest creaked downward, and Dad joined her on the sofa, tucking his arm around her and pulling her close. "Is it the holidays? Missing Mom?"

"Partly, I guess." The soft brush of his fleece half-zip against her cheek made her feel like a little girl again. She snuggled deeper into the crook of his shoulder. "How did you know, Daddy? When you and Mom fell in love, I mean."

"Can't say I remember anymore. Seems we just... knew." A chuckle rumbled through his chest. "I do recall one Sunday afternoon, though. We were sitting on her parents' sofa listening to the stereo, and I said, 'Peggy, how many kids do you want someday?' She said, 'Two, I think. A boy and a girl.' Then she winked at me and said, 'But we should probably get married first.' So just like that, we were engaged."

"And you had your boy and girl, just like Mom wanted."

"Yup, we did. The two most special kids ever in the world." He kissed the top of her head. "Dreaming of a family of your own…maybe with a certain young missionary pastor?"

"I don't know. Maybe." Heaving a sigh, she sat up and drew her knees beneath her. "But it's pointless. He's leaving for Jordan in a few weeks. I'll probably never see him again."

"Never say never," Dad said, tweaking her chin. "If he's the right one for you—"

"I know, I know. God will work out the details." But was God looking at the same calendar she used? What could possibly change in one month?

Better to set such thoughts aside and focus on what she could control, beginning with the jammies and cocoa calling her name. Tomorrow after church, she'd catch up on some things around the house and maybe spend a little time on the chamber website updates she'd been working on. Certainly, between her job at the chamber and the remaining tasks for the Christmas outreach project, she'd have more than enough to distract her from imagining an impossible future with Shaun.

You're getting too good at the distraction game, Brooke Willoughby. Too good at this pretense of control.

Because that was what it was, pure pretense. She could no more control her growing feelings for Shaun than she could order the sun to stop rising in the east.

Chapter Fourteen

"I'm glad you suggested the rosebushes, Emily." Taking a breather from their last-minute touches around the mobile home park office, Brooke dusted fragrant cedar mulch from her work gloves. "I'll have to come out next spring to see them in bloom."

"And your daffodils and tulips, too." Emily crumpled the plastic mulch bag they'd just emptied. "This is turning into a real showplace."

Brooke nodded, pride swelling her chest. As work had progressed over the committee's three workdays at the park, she'd noted a distinct change in their interactions with the residents. Many had welcomed them from the start, especially Mr. and Mrs. Paulos and their friends the Trans. But some families had been wary, as if needing to be convinced these strangers really would follow through on their promises to improve conditions.

Today, though, Brooke had overheard enthusiastic chatter all around the park as residents and volunteers worked side by side to complete the checklist of odd jobs and repairs. At the playground, younger children laughed

and chased each other as they climbed the monkey bars
and took turns on the new swing set.

And everyone was talking about the Christmas store,
now only two weeks away. Brooke could hardly wait to
see their expressions at their first glimpse of the myriad
gifts they could choose from, many donations perfectly
paired with the families' wish lists.

Emily gathered up her gardening tools. "Shall we go
check on the crew at the rec building?"

"Right behind you." Waving her on, Brooke pretended
to adjust one of the white river rocks they'd added to
decorate the flowerbed.

Truth was, she'd been doing her best all day to avoid
Shaun. When they'd spoken on the phone earlier in the
week to plan today's agenda, she'd kept the discussion
as light and friendly and to the point as she could. From
her perspective, it seemed as if he'd attempted to do the
same. Which meant they'd both come across as stilted
and phony.

In less than a month, all this would be behind them.
Shaun would be on a plane to Jordan, and Brooke could
start on a whole new batch of New Year's resolutions that
would likely be history by Valentine's Day.

Just what she needed, reminders of yet another holiday she'd just as soon skip.

Following the path toward the rec building, she hoped
to catch sight of Shaun before he noticed her so she could
make a quick detour. She spotted him with Mr. and Mrs.
Paulos and an older, nicely dressed gentleman she hadn't
seen around the park before. The Pauloses and the man
were smiling and talking animatedly. Hands tucked into
his jeans pockets, Shaun wore a thoughtful frown and
said little.

Mr. Zamora came her way with a bulging trash sack. "The hole in the Alanizes' ceiling has been patched. Now they will be ready for the arrival of the new baby."

"I'm sure they're getting excited." Brooke nodded toward the stranger across the way. "Do you know that man?"

"Ah, yes, that is the pastor from George and Mariam's church in Kerrville. He helped to sponsor them when they first came to the United States. He stops by to visit from time to time."

"That's nice." But it didn't explain why Shaun looked so serious. Maybe he wondered why the Pauloses' church hadn't done more for the families here. Brooke couldn't help wondering the same. "Has their church provided any other assistance?"

"Not to this great extent, certainly. It's a very small congregation, but they do what they can. Food drives, help with transportation, things like that." Mr. Zamora adjusted his grip on the trash bag. "Pardon me, I must dispose of this."

Across the way, Shaun shook hands with the pastor and Mr. Paulos, then started toward the rec building. He caught Brooke's eye and offered a brief smile. She wanted to ask him what the conversation had been about, but he'd already ducked through the door, apparently even more intent on avoiding her than she'd been about him.

None of her business anyway. Spying Emily near the playground with a couple of other committee members, she marched over to see what else might need attention. "How's it going? Anything left on our to-do list?"

"I think we're about to wrap it up," Emily said. "In

fact, we were just talking about everyone joining up at Casa Luis afterward for a celebratory dinner."

"Good idea." As long as well-meaning friends didn't subtly arrange for her to sit next to Shaun. "Let's split up and make one last check to make sure we haven't missed anything, and then we can head over."

"Why don't you see how Shaun's team is doing in the rec building while I track down everyone else?"

So much for avoidance. Brooke stretched her mouth into a semblance of a smile and started that way. Stepping inside, she gave her eyes a moment to adjust, then let her gaze sweep the newly painted walls and polished floor. Donations of shelving units, game tables, folding chairs and a new TV and DVD player made the space much more inviting. In the laundry room beyond, washers and dryers hummed, the flowery scents of detergent and fabric softener filling the air.

Shaun and another volunteer were filling a bookshelf from a large cardboard box on the floor between them.

"How's it going?" Brooke asked, trying to sound casual as she crossed the room.

Nearly dropping the handful of paperbacks he held, Shaun shot her a startled glance. "Uh, fine. Soon as we empty this box, we'll be done in here."

"Everything looks great." She shared Emily's suggestion about meeting at the Mexican restaurant for supper. When Shaun agreed, she checked the time on her phone. "It's four fifteen now. Think it would be safe to call in a reservation for five o'clock?"

"Sounds good." With a parting nod, Shaun went back to shelving books.

Guess he wasn't interested in talking.

When she met up with Emily a few minutes later,

they tallied the number of volunteers who were interested in dinner, and then Brooke phoned the restaurant. By four forty-five, people were getting into their cars to head over.

The Casa Luis manager had moved several tables together down the center of the noisy dining area. Working her way toward an empty seat, Brooke had to duck beneath a donkey piñata hanging from the ceiling. As she claimed a bright green chair, her hand landed on someone else's. "Oh, sorry—"

It was Shaun's. "Please, take it," he said, pulling his hand free. "I'll find another seat."

"No, you were here first. I can sit over…" She glanced down the length of the table, but all the chairs were quickly filling up. The only other empty spot was right next to this one.

Shaun cast her a wry grin. "It's déjà vu all over again."

"It certainly is." She couldn't help but smile at the reminder of the first time they'd met. Could the guy get any more charming?

Apparently, he could. With a courtly bow, he pulled out the chair for her. "At your service, Miss Willoughby."

Warmth creeping up her cheeks, she slid into the chair. With Shaun seated at her right, at least they weren't facing each other. The lively music playing over the speakers, combined with the din of other conversations, meant the most she'd have to worry about was making polite small talk.

Shaun usually hated being reduced to small talk, but in this situation it was probably for the best. The discussion with the Pauloses and their pastor still fresh in his mind, he needed time to think—although what was there to think about, really? His mind was made up. His course was set.

He was going back to Jordan. Period.

Sure, they'd gotten him pondering what it would be like if he stayed in the States to pastor a missions-minded church somewhere. Life could be as challenging for refugees coming to America as anywhere else. Immigrants with limited or no English skills needed long-term specialized assistance, a mentor to help them navigate the myriad details of starting over in a new country.

That was what the Pauloses' pastor had done for them. He'd expressed to Shaun how rewarding it had been, and George and Mariam had voiced their immense gratitude for his friendship and guidance through each phase of their transition to American life.

Even if he'd consider such a career change, God would have to lay the right opportunity in his lap—and soon, because the missions office had already arranged his flight to Amman and put him in touch with a British missionary couple offering him the extra room in their apartment.

But perhaps two or three years down the road, if he felt ready for something different by then…

Right, and two or three years from now, Brooke would have met someone else and moved on. She was too smart and too beautiful and too amazing a woman to waste time waiting for him.

"Shaun." Brooke tapped his arm. "The server's waiting to take your order."

"Sorry." He blinked several times and picked up the menu he hadn't bothered to look at. "Uh, the beef enchilada plate, please. And iced tea, unsweet—" Glancing over at Brooke, he was struck by a sudden impulse.

"Scratch that. Let's live on the wild side. Make it a sweet tea."

A surprised grin lit her face. "Wow, you *are* living dangerously. Sure you can handle it?"

The only thing he was sure about at the moment was how sorry he was to be leaving for the Middle East next month.

You don't have to go, a nagging voice whispered in his ear. *All you have to do is pick up the phone and tell Henry you changed your mind about accepting the position. You've done your time overseas. Nobody'd blame you if you stayed right here to find your own happiness.*

Nobody except himself. He'd long ago turned over control of his life to God, and if God wanted him in Jordan, that was where he'd go. Because the only true happiness was living in step with the Lord.

"You can change your mind, Shaun." Brooke was studying him with a concerned frown.

"Wha—what did you say?"

"You can change your mind about the sweet tea. I know you don't like it."

He choked out an embarrassed laugh, glad she hadn't really been reading his thoughts. "Hey, true Texans drink sweet tea, don't they? So it's about time I claimed my heritage." Even if Texas wouldn't be his place of residence much longer.

"Okay, then. But I'm going to get my cell phone ready so I can snap a photo of your lips puckering when you take that first sip."

Just then, the server returned with a tray of drinks. She set a dewy tumbler at Shaun's place. "Sweet tea, right?"

Brooke already had her phone out, a mischievous grin crinkling her cheeks. "Go ahead, Shaun, taste it."

By now, they had the attention of everyone at the table. Someone started a chant: "Taste. It. Taste. It." The others quickly joined in.

"All right, all right!" He peeled the wrapper off his straw and poked at the ice a few times while pretending to get up his nerve. Lifting the glass, he took a sip, then aimed an exaggerated grimace at Brooke while she snapped a photo.

"Yes! This is going on Facebook." She was already tapping icons on her phone.

"Hey, that wasn't part of the deal." Laughing, Shaun grabbed her wrist, hoping to stop her before she could complete the upload. His arm bumped the table, and ice rattled in the glasses.

"Careful, or you'll spill all our drinks." She stuffed the phone into her purse and shot him a smug smile. "No worries. I'll just do it after I get home later."

Did she have any idea what the sparkle in her eyes—even better, realizing he'd put it there—did to his pulse rate? Forget the sweet tea. He was getting deeper and deeper into dangerous territory every minute he spent with Brooke, and when he boarded the plane for Jordan in a few weeks, he wasn't sure his heart could stand the pain of leaving her behind.

"No, Henry, I'm not having second thoughts…exactly. Just investigating some options for the future." Shaun was back at Kent's after the Monday night outreach committee meeting, where sitting across the conference table from Brooke had reminded him all over again of his conversation with the Pauloses and their pastor on Saturday.

"I'm hearing some real uncertainty in your tone, Shaun." The missions director was known for his keen intuition. "If you're getting nudges from the Lord that Jordan isn't where you're called to go, then perhaps you should listen."

Nudges? Detour signs? Shaun couldn't be sure what these feelings were trying to tell him. "He hasn't specifically shown me I shouldn't go to Jordan, and since that's where He seems to be opening doors, I believe I'm supposed to walk through them. It's just…"

"Just what, son?"

Just that I'm falling in love, and I could never in a million years ask her to give up her life here to join me overseas. "Nothing. A local pastor I met the other day got me thinking, that's all."

Henry released a sharp breath. "Let's both keep praying about this. I'll talk to you again in a few days."

Ending the call, Shaun went to the fridge to pour himself a glass of milk. It had been a quiet week with Kent and Erin away on their honeymoon. They were expected back around noon tomorrow, and then Shaun would pack his things and move temporarily into Erin's house so the newlyweds could enjoy their privacy here at the ranch.

Skip ambled in from the living room, probably drawn by the clink of the cookie jar lid. "No way," Shaun said, wagging a finger at the dog. "I'm not sharing my sister's gingersnaps with you. Your master's getting home tomorrow, and you can take up the issue of special treats with him."

Although the old fella would probably get all kinds of treats and attention from Avery. When he'd seen his niece at church yesterday, she was practically glowing from her week with the Austins at Serenity Hills Guest Ranch. The kid was crazy about horses, and now that her new stepdad had horses she could ride every day, she'd probably become a skilled equestrian to rival her cousin Taylor.

Ranch life wasn't exactly Shaun's wheelhouse, however. He'd enjoyed his time here at Kent's, but if he hadn't had help this past week from Seth Austin and Kent's neighbor LeRoy, he'd have been in way over his head looking after Kent's cattle and horses.

Definitely time for the honeymooners to come home.

The next morning, he rose early for barn chores, and a few minutes after nine, LeRoy came by. He preferred driving his ancient pickup through the pastures to check on the cattle, so Shaun bounced along with him in the passenger seat. Not long after LeRoy left, Christina Austin and Marie Peterson, Seth's grandmother, arrived with welcome-home decorations for the house, along with a casserole and salad for the newlyweds' first meal together back home.

Skip and Gracie, Christina's service dog, made friends quickly, and off they trotted to the living room, probably to spread more dog hair all over Kent's recliner.

"Got a stepladder?" Christina asked as she unfolded a five-foot-long banner.

Shaun found one in the pantry and helped them hang the banner over the doorway between the kitchen and living room. "This looks great. My sister's really blessed to have such good friends."

"She's been a blessing to all of us." Christina passed him a strip of masking tape. "In fact, your whole family has been a welcome addition to Juniper Bluff. If Greg hadn't come out that day to ask about leasing Seth's horse for Taylor—"

"Exactly," Marie chimed in. "Thanks to your brother, Serenity Hills Guest Ranch is thriving again. And thanks to your sister, we have charming new decor in every cabin."

"And thanks to you and Brooke," Christina added, "the church's Christmas outreach is bigger and better than ever."

After securing the last piece of tape, Shaun climbed down from the ladder. "It's turned out well. Much better than I could have predicted when Emily first drafted us."

"She knew what she was doing," Christina said with a grin. "You and Brooke make a great team."

A team that would be history in less than two weeks. Swallowing over the knot in his chest, Shaun folded the stepladder. Before he could return it to its spot in the pantry, the flash of sunlight on a windshield drew his attention. He glanced out the window to see Erin's blue Camry coming up the driveway. "Uh-oh, they're back early."

"So much for the surprise." Marie gathered up the empty sacks from the food they'd brought while Christina packed their decorating supplies.

Seconds later, the door from the back porch flew open. A grinning Kent held Erin in his arms, preparing to carry her over the threshold. "Somebody get a camera ready so you can preserve this moment for posterity."

Christina whipped out her cell phone. "Ready when you are!"

Laughing, Erin grabbed the door frame to keep Kent from stepping through. "Wait, is this my good side? Maybe we should switch."

"Nothin' doin'. My knees are about to buckle as it is." A total exaggeration, since Shaun's petite sister couldn't weigh more than a hundred pounds soaking wet, and Kent regularly hefted hay bales and feed sacks at least that heavy. "Besides," Kent said, his gaze warming, "my gorgeous wife doesn't have a bad side."

They shared a kiss then, almost as if they'd forgotten they had an audience.

"Camera's rolling, guys," Christina reminded them.

"Oh, yeah." Kent faked a stumble, eliciting a shriek from Erin. Once inside the kitchen, though, he acted as if he didn't want to put her down.

Watching them, Shaun felt a wet nose beneath his palm. He found Gracie staring up at him with big brown eyes that spoke sympathy, understanding and so much more than he ever realized a dog could communicate. When Christina cast him a meaningful look of her own, he figured he hadn't been as good at disguising his current emotional state as he'd hoped. Envy hadn't often been a problem for him, but seeing Kent and Erin so happy, today he felt positively green.

Chapter Fifteen

The following Saturday, the outreach committee met at the church to begin organizing the donations that had come in for the Christmas store. Pastor Terry had arranged for them to have exclusive access to the fellowship hall through the day of the event, and with table groupings laid out from one end of the room to the other, items could be displayed by category as well as by family wish lists.

Brooke strode the aisles, recording the voucher price for each item on her tablet computer and making sure gifts that matched the families' personal requests were earmarked especially for them.

Turning down the next row, she met Shaun rolling a tiny bike with training wheels and couldn't hold back a teasing grin. "Isn't that a little small for you?"

He looked at the bike, then at Brooke, in feigned confusion. "Really? I was thinking of trading in my beat-up old car for this spiffy set of wheels."

"It would definitely be an improvement." Why was it so much fun to wisecrack with him? "But I think the little girl who asked for a new bicycle would be very disappointed."

"Guess you're right." He cast her a sheepish smile. "Wouldn't fit in the airplane overhead anyway."

The reminder that he'd be leaving soon hit hard. Biting her lip, she scrolled down her tablet list until she found the bike. "What did we decide on for the voucher price?"

"Twenty credits, wasn't it?"

"Right. And be sure to tag it for the Alaniz family." Looking past Shaun, she caught Emily motioning her over. "Must keep moving. See you later."

As she drew near, Emily held up two adult-size down jackets. "Someone just dropped these off. Aren't they nice?"

"Those are exactly what the Trans asked for." Brooke consulted her list and entered a description of the jackets. "Five credits each?"

"Sounds perfect." Laying the jackets on a nearby table, Emily pulled two labels from her pocket and uncapped her felt-tip pen. "I'll put Mr. and Mrs. Tran's names on them right now."

By midafternoon, most of the donations had been sorted, tagged and arranged. Anything that came in over the next few days would be easy enough to add to the displays. Surveying the room, Brooke breathed out a pleased sigh.

Shaun came up beside her. "Looks great. And I'll be the first to admit, your computerized record-keeping system beats my humble ballpoint pen and steno pad hands down."

"Glad to see you're coming to appreciate the wonders of technology." She smirked. "Even if I can't say the same about your regard for sweet tea."

"I finished the entire glass, if you recall. Although that night I did brush my teeth for twenty minutes to ward off any cavities."

"Very funny." She gave him a playful jab in the arm.

He caught her wrist, a mischievous glint in his eye, and for a moment they both froze. His glance fell to her lips and lingered there briefly before he released her arm. "Looks like everyone's heading out." He sounded as breathless as she felt. "Guess we should get the lights and lock up."

Shaun walked with her as far as her car and waited while she put her things inside. "I've got plenty of free time now that I'm staying in town. If there's anything you need me to do during the day this week, let me know."

"Thanks. How are the newlyweds, by the way? I caught a glimpse of Erin yesterday on her way to work at WE Design."

"Couldn't be happier." He glanced away, an odd sadness briefly clouding his eyes. When he looked at Brooke again, a stiff smile returned. "Better get going. Need to stop at the supermarket to pick up something for supper."

"My dad's grilling steaks tonight," she burst out before he could walk away. "Tripp and Diana are coming over, too. You're welcome to join us."

He shrugged. "Thanks, but…I'd hate to impose."

"You wouldn't be." She could do this friendship thing, if that was all the Lord wanted for her. Besides, she'd like to hope Shaun would stay in touch via email or Skype while overseas. "Please. Dad always cooks extra, and you're going to eat anyway, so why not with friends?"

After a thoughtful pause, he quirked a grin. "Steak, you said? What time?"

Her heart threw in an extra beat. "Follow me over now if you like."

A few minutes later, he pulled in behind her in the driveway. A car Brooke didn't recognize was already parked at the curb, and she had a funny feeling who the owner might be. *You can do this, too, Brooke Willoughby.*

Shaun's car door moaned pitifully as he shoved it closed with his hip. Glancing at Brooke, he grimaced. "Told you I should have traded for the bike."

Having him to joke with would certainly make it easier to get through what could turn out to be a painfully uncomfortable evening. "Come on inside. I can already smell the grill firing up."

Her instincts had been correct. The lovely silver-haired Lydia stood at the stove stirring a pot of something savory. "Hi, Brooke. Your father's on the patio getting the charcoal started."

She offered her friendliest smile. "Smells good in here. What's cooking?"

"It's my special Tuscan white beans." Lydia glanced over at Shaun. "Oh, hello. You're the missionary pastor, aren't you?"

"Shaun O'Grady." He stepped forward to accept Lydia's handshake.

"I've been hearing so much about what you and Brooke are doing for the Christmas outreach. Jim and I have both signed up to help man the store next Saturday."

"Thanks, we appreciate it."

"Shaun, let me take your jacket," Brooke said, suddenly needing a reason to get out of the kitchen. Even though her mother had never lived in this house, it still felt wrong to see another woman at the stove and to hear her call Brooke's father by his given name.

Shaun followed her into the front hallway. "So that's Lydia. She seems nice."

"Yeah, she does." She found an empty hanger in the coat closet and hung up Shaun's jacket. "And I'm being ridiculous."

"No, you're not. There's no timetable for grieving." He took her hand, his touch warmly comforting, and the same look she'd seen in his eyes less than an hour ago returned, this time even more intense.

He wants to kiss me.

She wanted to kiss him.

But would it be for the right reasons?

Then she stopped wondering, because it was going to happen anyway. His left hand crept around her back as he drew her close, his lips gently meeting hers.

The kiss was brief but filled with meaning. Their foreheads still touching, he murmured, "I'm sorry. I had no right."

"Don't apologize. I've been wanting to kiss you for the longest time."

A soft chuckle vibrated in his throat. "Then the feeling was mutual." Brows drawn together, he edged a step back. "But how do we do this? I'll be clear across the ocean, and you'll be here in Juniper Bluff."

"I don't know, Shaun." She turned away, arms crossed tightly across her chest. "I'm not even sure we should try."

Behind her, there was silence, then the click of the closet door and the rustle of fabric. Wearing his jacket again, Shaun stepped past her toward the front door. Without looking at her, he reached for the knob. "Thanks for the dinner invitation, but I think it's best if I don't stay. I've already taken advantage, and the last thing I want is to make this more painful for us than it already is."

"Shaun—"

"We'll talk again in a few days. Good night, Brooke."

The door whispered closed, and he was gone.

Kissing her? What had he been thinking? Sure, might as well get a taste of what he'd be missing for the rest of his life.

Big, big, big mistake.

He yanked the car door open, his teeth clenching at the screech of the hinges. If he had any sense, on the day he left for Jordan, he should drive this piece of junk straight off the nearest cliff, then call a taxi to take him to the airport.

Jamming the key into the ignition, he gave it a twist. The engine grumbled a few times but wouldn't start. He pumped the gas pedal and tried again. A grinding noise and then nothing.

"Car trouble?" Tripp Willoughby's face appeared at his window.

Shaun cranked down the glass. "Usually takes a few tries." He turned the key again. Same result.

"Pop the hood. I'll take a look."

Probably useless, but Shaun needed to get going. He pulled the release lever. Tripp poked around under the hood and then had him give it another try. This time there was only a series of dull clicks.

"Could be the starter." Tripp slammed the hood closed and came back to the window. "Sorry, that's the extent of my auto mechanic know-how. Were you just leaving? Need a lift somewhere?"

"That's okay. I'll call for a tow." Shaun already had his cell phone out. As badly as he'd already messed things up, he wouldn't inconvenience Brooke or her family any further.

Tripp gave a doubtful frown. "It's getting pretty chilly out here. Why don't you come inside to wait?"

"No, thanks." Glancing at his phone, he noticed the display registered three missed calls and a voice mail. All had come in while they'd been organizing the Christmas store. "Y'all are getting ready for dinner, and I've got some calls to return anyway. I'll see you in church tomorrow."

"Okay, but if the tow truck's running late, there's always room for one more at the table." Tripp waved as he started toward the porch, where Diana waited on the front step with a large serving bowl.

If only they wouldn't mention to Brooke that he was still sitting out here in a stalled car. The way they'd parted, she probably wasn't ready to see him again anytime soon.

He made the call to the auto club and was told a truck would be there in about twenty minutes, which, in Shaun's experience, probably meant more like an hour. Settling in for a long wait, he scrolled through the missed calls, all from the same number but with no name attached. The caller had left the voice mail after the third attempt, but when Shaun tried to listen to the message, the sound was garbled. The only words that came through clearly were *church* and *mobile home park*. Most likely someone with a donation for the Christmas outreach. Redialing the number led to another bad connection, so he'd have to trust they'd eventually call back.

Amazingly, the tow truck showed up fifteen minutes

later. "Your lucky day," the driver said as he prepared to winch Shaun's car onto the truck. "Just wrapped up a service call around the corner, so I came right over."

Shaun didn't believe in luck, but he wouldn't put it past the Lord to bail him out of what could have grown into an extremely awkward evening.

He had the driver drop him at Erin's old house before delivering the car to the auto mechanic in town, where it would probably sit in the parking lot until the garage opened on Monday morning. Guess he wouldn't be seeing Tripp—or anyone else—in church tomorrow.

And, since he'd never made it to the supermarket either, he'd be dining on canned soup and stale crackers. During his missionary service, he'd survived many times on much less filling or nutritious meals. But a steak sure would have tasted good, especially with his beautiful dinner companion—

Don't go there. Best not to think about Brooke at all. Like forgetting her was even remotely possible.

I'm not even sure we should try, she'd said, which had to mean she'd been fighting feelings for him as hard as he'd been resisting his toward her.

Bile rose in his throat, simmering anger toward God for placing him in such an impossible situation. "I've done my best for You, haven't I?" he shouted at the ceiling. "I trusted You, turned my entire life over to Your control in full obedience to wherever Your call has taken me. So my reward is a broken heart because I've fallen in love with a woman I can never have? Thanks a lot!"

Hissing and spattering sounded behind him. He whirled around to find his soup had boiled over. "Great," he muttered, turning off the stove. "Just great."

Good thing he knew the Lord was big enough and gracious enough to handle his angry outburst. He also knew better than to blame God for his supper being ruined. He poured what was left of the soup into a bowl, grabbed a spoon and carried the meager meal to the table. Bowing his head, he offered up a silent apology and began the Lord's Prayer, only to pause over the words, *Give us this day our daily bread.*

This day. Today. Jesus hadn't said to ask for tomorrow's bread or next month's or next year's.

Shaun had come to Juniper Bluff to rest and recover after an exhausting three years of service in Ethiopia while also listening for God's direction for what came next. And each day since, God had supplied exactly what he needed, even if it hadn't always seemed so.

Words from a treasured psalm arose in his thoughts: *But I trusted in thee, O Lord: I said, Thou art my God. My times are in thy hand.*

That wasn't going to change. Not tomorrow or next month or next year.

Dinner with Lydia turned out not to be nearly as uncomfortable as Brooke had feared. For one thing, her attempts at politeness gave her something to focus on besides regret over how things had ended with Shaun. Even with no hope of anything ever coming of these feelings between them, they still had to work together finishing the Christmas outreach. Besides, she valued Shaun's friendship and wanted to keep it, no matter how far away his missionary work took him.

As they were getting dinner on the table, she'd heard rumbling out front and had peeked out the kitchen window to see a tow truck loading Shaun's car. Then she'd felt even worse, knowing he'd been waiting outside with a stalled car all that time. Tripp mentioned he'd tried to help, even invited Shaun to come in and join them for dinner. Brooke kept it to herself that she was the reason Shaun had been in such a hurry to leave.

Now, after an exhausting day and an emotionally charged evening, she was ready for some alone time. After supper, she sent everyone to the living room to visit, insisting she'd take care of the kitchen cleanup. She'd just started loading the dishwasher when Lydia peeked in.

"You were on your feet all day at the church. You must let me help." Lydia picked up a dishcloth and began wiping counters.

"Thanks, but I'm doing okay." Scouring a stubborn spot on a serving platter, Brooke smiled over her shoulder. "Washing dishes is therapeutic."

"Cooking is my therapy. Even after my three sons grew up and left home, I couldn't seem to stop cooking for an army. My late husband used to tease me about all the leftovers…" Her voice trailed off.

Apparently, leftovers were still an issue, considering how much remained of Lydia's delicious white beans, and they'd all eaten their fair share. "Dad says your kids all live elsewhere now. Do you see them often?"

"Not nearly often enough." Sighing, Lydia rinsed out the dishcloth. "Which is why I'm so grateful for my church family at Shepherd of the Hills."

"Dad's certainly been having fun with the seniors group. He's needed something like that." A knot formed in Brooke's throat. She set the last plate in the dishwasher, then started the wash cycle. Turning, she leaned against the counter and admitted the truth she'd been avoiding. "He's needed a friend like you."

"We've filled a need for each other. Brooke, dear..." Lydia stepped closer, compassion and understanding in her eyes. "I've grown very fond of your father, but I'd never want you to feel I'm trying to fill your mother's place in his life."

"I know. It's just...this has been a difficult year, and I haven't always handled my grief in the most productive ways."

"Oh, honey, come here." Lydia pulled her into a spontaneous hug.

Finding herself wrapped in the arms of a gentle and caring older woman brought more comfort than Brooke could have imagined. Surprisingly, it was exactly what she needed, what she'd been missing ever since her mother's death. Cleansing tears flowed, and she clung to Lydia for all she was worth.

Footsteps sounded as Dad, Tripp and Diana hurried in from the living room. "Brooke?" Concern filled her father's tone. "Honey, are you all right?"

"She'll be fine," Lydia whispered, stroking Brooke's back. "Every once in a while, a gal just needs a good cry."

She sniffled and straightened, embarrassed to discover she'd left a streak of black mascara on Lydia's blouse. Diana handed her a fistful of tissues, and she blotted her cheeks with one hand while dabbing Lydia's blouse with the other. "I'm so sorry. I hope it comes out."

"Don't you worry about it. Now go sit down, and I'll start water for tea. Do you have chamomile?"

"I'll get it." Giving Brooke's shoulder a pat, Diana opened the pantry.

Tripp pulled out a chair for her at the table, and her father guided her into it. She felt silly for causing such a fuss, but she also felt as if a huge burden had been lifted from her heart. Even though her mother was gone, she wasn't alone. God had surrounded her with people who loved her and cared about her. People she could turn to and trust to stand firm with her, even when everything else in her world spun horribly out of control.

Chapter Sixteen

Days later, Brooke still felt buoyed by the comforting hug Lydia had offered Saturday evening. Lydia's arm's weren't Mom's, but Brooke had found peace in her embrace nonetheless. Peace…and strength. Because she'd need every bit of both as the Christmas outreach project ended and Shaun left for Jordan.

With several things going on at the chamber of commerce, including a Christmas open house and end-of-year wrap-up meetings for several chamber committees, she couldn't easily break away to offer much help with final preparations for the Christmas store. By Friday, though, things began to slow down. Her final obligation of the week was a come and go luncheon buffet hosted by Tripp and his veterinary partner, Robert Ingram. Attending was as much business as pleasure, since she and Inez were there as representatives of the chamber of commerce, but she'd have been there anyway, because she always enjoyed seeing her brother in his element. Tripp had definitely found his niche here in small-town Juniper Bluff, obvious from the appreciation bestowed by his many clients.

Erin and Kent stopped in as Brooke was finishing her last egg roll. Spotting her, Erin made her way over. "We were just at the church to see how things were going with the store. I can't believe how many donations have come in."

"The community has really come through for us." Brooke dabbed her lips with a napkin. "I'm on my way over to help as soon as I leave here."

"Oh, good. Shaun will be glad to see you. He was looking a little frazzled trying to keep track of everything."

Brooke could guess why. She wiggled a brow. "Still trying to get by with his trusty steno pad and ballpoint pen?"

"Actually, he bought himself a tablet computer this week, and he's still figuring it out." Leaning closer, Erin lowered her voice. "He offered to pick up Avery after school on Wednesday and then spent two hours having her show him how to use it."

Laughter burst from Brooke's throat, and she nearly dropped her plate. "Maybe you *can* teach an old dog new tricks."

"Don't count on it. As we were leaving, I'm pretty sure he was about to trash the tablet and dig out his steno pad again."

"Then maybe I should hurry on over." She set her empty plate on a nearby tray, then said her goodbyes and headed to the church.

She found Shaun, Emily and a few other volunteers huddled around a large cardboard crate near the fellowship hall entrance. Whatever the box held had them riveted.

She edged closer. "Uh, guys, what's going on?"

Shaun turned with a start, then stepped aside. A quirky grin flashed across his face, then immediately vanished. "Maybe you'd better have a look for yourself."

Warily, she peered into the box. "A *kitten*?"

"Complete with litter pan, scratching post, food and bowls." Shaun thrust a scribbled page from his steno pad in front of her. Apparently, Erin was right about his giving up on the tablet computer. "I can't find a kitten on anyone's wish list from the mobile home park. Know anything about this?"

"Sorry, not a clue." The mewing kitten stretched its little gray paws toward Brooke, and she couldn't resist scooping it up into her arms. With the furry creature nuzzling her chin, she cast questioning glances at Shaun and the other volunteers. "Was it left here like it was supposed to be a donation?"

Emily reached over to stroke the kitten's head. "Seems so. But it must be meant for someone really special." Her eyes twinkled. "Shaun, wouldn't you agree?"

"Someone very special, yes." He was looking straight at Brooke, myriad emotions reflected in his gaze.

The kitten now purred loudly, the vibration tickling Brooke's neck. "Okay," she said, sensing some mischief afoot. "Somebody better tell me what's going on right now."

Looking entirely too smug, Emily shooed the other volunteers away, leaving Brooke and Shaun alone. He tilted his head and offered a boyish smile. "After Thanksgiving with all the animals at the assisted living center, I got the idea that you might enjoy having a kitten to keep you company. So I talked to your brother, and he connected me with a cat rescue person——"

She gasped. "Tripp was in on this, too?"

"I had to be sure the kitten was healthy and had all its shots."

To her horror, she realized she was already growing attached. "And you decided I needed a cat...why, exactly?"

"Because you have so much love to give." His tone mellowed to match his expression, and it brought a clench to her throat. "There's no right time or right way to say this, Brooke. I just want you to know how much our time together has meant to me. Whatever happens, wherever life takes us, I pray only God's very best for you. And I thought..." He sighed and shoved his hands into his pockets. "I hoped this little ball of fur would help you think kindly of me after I leave."

Heart aching, she shook her head at him. "Shaun, I'll always think kindly of you. How could I not?"

His shoulders rose and fell in a tired shrug, and he stared past her as if searching for words. His voice barely a whisper, he said, "You don't know how badly I've wished things were different—that I could stay, or that you'd come with me. But I can't, and you can't—"

"Shaun... Shaun." The kitten nearly crushed between them, she drew him into a hug. "I'm so sorry for being so negative the other night. Only the Lord knows what the future holds for us, and if there's any way we could make this work, I *do* want to try. Shaun, I..." She swallowed back tears, and instead of telling him she loved him, she showed him with her kiss.

Was this really happening—promise and hope from the woman he fell more in love with every day?

From the woman he'd be saying goodbye to much sooner than his breaking heart could bear?

The kitten squirmed between them. He pulled away to give the poor thing some breathing room while he fought to bring his runaway emotions under control.

Control? Not much chance as long as she stood this close, love beaming from her eyes like a lighthouse in a storm.

"I won't ask you to go with me," he said, cupping her cheek. A weak chuckle escaped. "I know you better than that."

She looked hurt, and yet her sad smile said she knew he was right. "I could visit sometimes. And your assignment isn't forever...is it?"

This was killing him. He didn't want to be parted from her for even a day. Hadn't this past week proven as much? Longing for any reason to call or see her, he'd moped around Erin's old house like a lovesick teenager while counting the minutes until he could be with her today.

Instead of answering her question, he turned his attention to the kitten. "What are you going to name him?"

"It's a boy?"

"According to your brother."

"Hmm, I'll have to think about it." Her chest heaved in a hiccupping breath, and she smiled as she flicked away a tear. "I can't believe you got me a cat."

There didn't seem to be much else to say. Nothing that would change things, anyway. Then Shaun's phone buzzed in his pocket. He shrugged an apology and took a few steps away to answer. The same number that had been calling all week appeared on the display. "Hello?... Hello?"

Still nothing but garbled sounds. He shoved the phone back into his pocket.

Brooke looked up from placing the kitten in its box. "No one there?"

"Weird. Whoever it is can't seem to get through, and I haven't been able to call them back, either."

"Probably one of those sales robocalls. You should block the number."

He hiked a brow. "You can do that?"

"What are we going to do with you, Shaun O'Grady? Hand me your phone." Her exasperated eye roll was exactly the reaction he'd hoped for to lighten the mood. After pressing some buttons, she returned the phone. "There, all taken care of. I heard all about your niece trying to teach you how to use your new tablet."

"Speaking of which, guess we should get busy logging the last of the donations."

At least today's tasks were much less complicated than figuring out how to manage their relationship over time and distance. Shaun only knew, now more than ever, that they had to give their love a chance.

Three hours later, they declared the Christmas store ready for opening day. While Emily and the others shut things down, Shaun helped Brooke get the kitten box out to her car and secure it in the backseat. With the day's work done and nothing else between them, the awkwardness returned.

"Guess I'll see you in the morning," he said.

"Bright and early." Her eyes glimmered in the fading sunlight. "I can't wait to see everyone's faces when they come to shop for their gifts."

"Me, too." And sharing the experience with Brooke would make it all the sweeter.

They shared a quick good-night kiss that left Shaun

aching for more and asking God for the millionth time to somehow find a way to keep Brooke in his life.

In no hurry to return to an empty house, he lingered in town for a bit, then stopped at the supermarket deli for supper. Afterward, he opted for an early night so he'd be fully rested for the big day tomorrow, but even so, he tossed and turned more than he slept.

Two strong cups of coffee got him out the door the next morning—that, plus knowing he'd be spending the day with Brooke. Just as well they'd both be preoccupied with making sure the Christmas store ran smoothly. Less time to dwell on the complications surrounding a *very* long-distance relationship.

When he arrived, Brooke had just sent the first couple of volunteers to their stations. Checking the time, she narrowed one eye. "You are two minutes late, Pastor O'Grady." A crooked smile belied her crisp tone. "Don't tell me that rusty thing you call a car broke down again?"

Couldn't use that excuse. The car had been running fine since he'd gotten it back from the garage on Tuesday. "Rough night. Sorry."

Her smile turned sympathetic. "Yeah. Same here." She consulted her tablet. "I've got you down as a floater. That still okay?"

"Right. I'll do spot checks and be around to help if anyone's having problems at their station." He surveyed the fellowship hall, once again impressed with the array of donations and how attractively everything was organized.

As more volunteers arrived, Brooke gave them their assignments. By nine thirty everyone was in place, and stirrings in the corridor indicated the mobile home park families waited excitedly for the doors to open. After one more check, Brooke nodded to Shaun to invite the families in.

Awe and delight filled each face as the park residents got their first glimpse of the Christmas store. First stop was the check-in table, where Emily and Alma were stationed to hand each family their vouchers. Those who had submitted wish lists were shown where to find those items. They could also choose from any of the other gifts on display.

Once the shopping began and things appeared to be running smoothly, a little of Shaun's tension lifted. Glimpsing George and Mariam Paulos admiring the new stand mixer Mariam had requested, he recalled her *maamoul*, those delicious date cookies she was now baking for Diana at the doughnut shop. It was a bittersweet reminder that his departure for Jordan was barely two weeks away.

Mariam spotted him and waved him over, her smile ebullient. "This is so much nicer than I expected—so many fancy settings to learn! How can we ever thank you for doing all this for us?"

"It was a labor of love." The truth. He gripped both Mariam's hands.

"Our pastor sends you greetings," George said. "Have you spoken yet with the couple he referred to you?"

Puzzled, Shaun shook his head. "Was I supposed to— Wait, I've gotten several calls from an unfamiliar number, but it's always a bad connection. Do you know what this is about?"

"A pastor at another church in Kerrville is—"

Before he could finish, Emily rushed over, a middle-aged man and woman following close behind. "There you are, Shaun. These nice folks just arrived looking for you. They say they've been trying to call but can't get through."

More confused than ever, Shaun turned to the couple. "I'm Shaun O'Grady. How can I help you?"

"We hope you mean that sincerely," the man replied, "because we are here to discuss how you can do exactly that."

Brooke marched over to the check-in table. "Alma, do you know who those people are?" She'd seen the unfamiliar couple arrive, and moments later Emily had escorted them directly to Shaun.

"Said their name was Harper or Horton or something like that. They drove over from Kerrville."

"And they came here looking for Shaun?"

"So they said."

Whom did Shaun know in Kerrville? Whatever this was about, the couple certainly had Shaun's attention. After a few minutes of intense conversation, he motioned toward a side door leading to the church offices. As he showed the couple out, he happened to glance in Brooke's direction, his jaw clenched in a look that gave her chills. In the next instant, he disappeared through the exit behind his visitors.

Mouth agape, Brooke stared after them, half tempted to follow and find out if everything was okay. Before she could, one of the volunteers tapped her arm. With a final glance toward the side door, she turned and strove for a smile.

It was Kelly, the nurse practitioner from the pharmacy. "We have a little problem over here. Can you help us sort it out?"

"Sure, what's up?"

"Mrs. Alaniz misplaced her vouchers, and she's distraught that she won't be able to buy the bicycle her little girl asked for."

"Oh, no, we can't have that." Brooke hurried through the aisles to where the very pregnant Elena Alaniz was frantically searching through her purse. "Elena, it's okay. We can replace your vouchers."

"You can? Oh, thank you!" Choking back tears, the woman clutched Brooke's hand. "Marisol wants her bike more than anything."

"And she's going to get it, don't you worry." Consulting her tablet, Brooke had Kelly write down on a slip of paper how many voucher credits they'd issued the Alaniz family. "Here's how much you can spend today, so go ahead and do your shopping, and I'll have another set of vouchers printed for you by the time you're ready to check out."

An adjacent Sunday school room had been set up as the Christmas store business office. Brooke settled in at the computer, and a few minutes later the printer spit out duplicates of the missing vouchers. Returning to the fellowship hall, she found Elena browsing one of the other display tables. "Here you go. You're all set."

After accepting the young mother's grateful hug, she glanced around for Shaun but didn't find him. The look on his face just before he'd slipped out had her stomach churning with worry. Could these people be connected with his missions organization? Had they come to tell him he must leave much sooner than planned?

In the middle of handling another small crisis, she caught a glimpse of him back on the floor assisting one of the families with their purchases. Something about his expression had changed. He didn't appear troubled or upset, just extremely preoccupied.

As families completed their selections and began the checkout process, things got busier than ever. The line at the cashier station lengthened, and then the shoppers had to get their selections to the gift wrapping room without spoiling the surprise for the recipients. Several times, Brooke's duties brought her near enough to brush arms with Shaun, but neither of them had time to stop. She was going crazy wanting to find out who those visitors were and why they so urgently needed to talk with him.

It was nearly two o'clock before the last family from the mobile home park packed up their gifts and loaded them into their car. Dead on her feet, Brooke carried a stack of receipts to the office and sat down at the computer to log the final batch of voucher purchases. Only a few of the donations remained unclaimed, and those they would deliver next week to the Salvation Army so that others might be blessed in some small way.

The entries complete, Brooke nudged the computer to one side and leaned forward to rest her head on her forearms. A five-minute nap, that was all she asked…

"Brooke? Can we talk a minute?"

Her head snapped up. At the sight of Shaun's smiling face, all the questions she'd ached all day to ask him now died on her tongue. "Hi."

"Hi, yourself." He circled the table and pulled up a chair facing her. A disconcerting grin skewed his lips as he reached for her hand. "I need to ask you something."

A distant part of her sleepy brain registered that he was holding her left hand, his thumb stroking gently across her ring finger. Was she dreaming? Because if he were to suddenly drop to one knee… "Wh-what is it?"

He laughed softly. "I'm not sure you're awake enough to answer."

"No, I'm awake." She scrubbed her free hand across her eyes, probably smearing her mascara in the process. Her head was finally clearing. "Does this have anything to do with those people you were with this morning?"

"It does. And I have to make a decision right away, but it's a big one, and I need to know how it would affect us."

"Us?" A swallow caught in her throat. "Shaun, what do you mean?"

"That couple, Mr. and Mrs. Harper, chair the call committee for a church in Kerrville. They're the ones who have been trying to reach me all week."

"Call committee. That's what they do when they're looking for a new pastor, right?" She wasn't getting this. "So why—"

"Because," he said, claiming her other hand, "their congregation is sensing the Lord's urging to develop a refugee outreach ministry, but with their current pastor planning to retire soon, they've been praying for God to lead them to the right person. When the Pauloses' pastor told them about me—" He held her gaze. "Brooke, they've invited me to interview for the pastorate."

Stunned, she lowered her eyes to their entwined hands. "But you're going to Jordan."

"I've already called my director and told him what's happening. He agrees God's hand is at work here, and if the call is extended, he's confident he'll find someone else for the Jordan position."

"So…so you'd be staying? In Juniper Bluff?"

"Or Kerrville. But it's only a few minutes down the road. I'd still be close by…until…" He hadn't stopped caressing her ring finger. "Whatever happens, Brooke, I want you in my future. I'm falling more in love with you every day, more than I ever imagined possible."

"Oh, Shaun, I love you, too!" She launched herself into his arms, and as he lowered his lips to hers, she offered silent thanks to God for the precious gift of love He'd brought her this Christmas.

Epilogue

"Normally we would have avoided scheduling this interview on Christmas Eve." Mr. Harper sat opposite Shaun at the oblong conference table. "However, we understand your need for a quick decision."

"Thank you, sir. If the committee should decide I'm not the best fit, I could still go forward with the missions assignment I was offered in Jordan." Hands clenched under the table, Shaun sent up yet another silent prayer. He wanted this pastorate, and not only because it would mean staying in Texas with Brooke. The more he'd learned about the church's vision for refugee assistance, the more certain he was about wanting to be a part of it.

One by one, the members of the call committee questioned him on everything from his family connections, to his missionary background and spiritual life, to his hopes for the future.

His greatest hope waited just beyond the conference room door. Brooke had driven over to Kerrville with him to offer moral support and also because she wanted to be the first to know the call committee's decision.

More than two hours later, the interview ended, and

Mr. Harper asked Shaun to wait outside while the committee deliberated.

Brooke sprang to her feet as he stepped into the corridor. "Well? How did it go?"

Exhausted, he drew her into a hug. "Pretty well, I think. I felt the Holy Spirit with me the whole time." With a smile and a kiss on her cheek, he whispered, "Felt your prayers, too."

"And there were plenty of them." She slipped an arm around his waist. "There's a coffee machine in the room across the hall. Want some while we wait?"

"Only if it's decaf. My pulse is already going ninety miles an hour."

They'd barely filled two mugs when the conference room door opened. Mr. and Mrs. Harper crossed into the break room, and their beaming faces conveyed their answer before they even said a word.

"Pastor O'Grady," Mr. Harper said, "the vote was unanimous. We would be honored and blessed to have you accept the call as head minister of Hope of Glory Church."

His coffee forgotten, Shaun gripped the man's hand and shook it firmly. "Yes! I accept, and thank you."

This time, Brooke was invited to join Shaun in the conference room. She'd soon be a part of this team, too—very soon, if Shaun had his way. Then he paused, closed his eyes and mentally released it all to the Lord, because God had shown him again and again that His ways were higher, His plans better, His answers to prayer more wonderfully satisfying than anything Shaun could devise for himself.

With the preliminary details laid out and an agreed-upon starting date of February 1, Shaun and Brooke said their goodbyes. A bright winter sun shone on them as they walked arm in arm across the parking lot. Reaching the car, Shaun felt a whoop of joy bubbling up inside him. "This is the second happiest day of my life."

"Oh, really?" Arm tucked in his, Brooke tilted her head. "What's the happiest?"

"That day hasn't happened yet."

She beamed up at him. "Something tells me it's going to be *my* happiest day ever, too!" With a sudden gasp, she said, "I've just thought of the perfect name for my—*our*—kitten. What do you think of 'Merry'?"

"As in 'Merry Christmas'? It's perfect!"

* * * * *

If you enjoyed Their Christmas Prayer*,*
look for Myra Johnson's earlier books

Rancher for the Holidays
Her Hill Country Cowboy
Hill Country Reunion
The Rancher's Redemption

Available now from Love Inspired!

Find more great reads at
www.LoveInspired.com

Dear Reader,

As human beings, we naturally want to be in control, to make our plans and see them through. This was certainly the struggle Brooke and Shaun faced. Each in their own way, they had to learn how to let go of their own agendas and turn everything over to God.

Releasing control can be a struggle for me, too. I think I know what's best for me, and my tendency is to push ahead until I make it happen...or make the situation worse. The problem is, I'm not God. He sees the whole picture—past, present and future—while all I can see is my own little part of it. I really *don't* know what's best for me, after all.

Yes, letting go can be scary. But as Shaun understood, all God asks of us is that we take each step in faith. If we're trusting in Him, He won't let us stray. The path won't always be easy, and we may face periods of discouragement, but God's best is always worth waiting for, no matter how long it takes.

Thank you so much for joining me in this return to Juniper Bluff for Brooke and Shaun's story. The Texas Hill Country is very special to me, and I'm delighted to call it home once again.

I love to hear from readers, so please contact me through my website, www.MyraJohnson.com, or write to me c/o Love Inspired Books, 195 Broadway, New York, NY 10007.

Keeping all my readers in my prayers,
Myra

COMING NEXT MONTH FROM
Love Inspired®

Available October 15, 2019

THE CHRISTMAS COURTSHIP
by Emma Miller

Caught up in a scandal in her Amish community, Phoebe Miller moves to her cousin's farm in Delaware hoping for forgiveness and a fresh start. The last thing Phoebe expects is to fall for bachelor Joshua Miller. But can their love survive her secret?

HER AMISH CHRISTMAS CHOICE
Colorado Amish Courtships • by Leigh Bale

Inheriting a shop from her grandfather could solve all of Julia Rose's problems—if Martin Hostetler will renovate it. As an *Englischer*, romance with the Amish man is almost impossible, especially with her mother against it. But Martin and his faith are slowly starting to feel like home...

WESTERN CHRISTMAS WISHES
by Brenda Minton and Jill Kemerer

Homecomings bring love for two cowboys in these holiday novellas, where a woman gets more than she bargained for with a foster teen to care for and a handsome cowboy next door, and a bachelor finds an instant family with a single mom and her little girl.

THE TEXAN'S SURPRISE RETURN
Cowboys of Diamondback Ranch • by Jolene Navarro

Returning home with amnesia years after he was declared dead, Xavier De La Rosa is prepared to reconnect with family—but he's stunned to learn he has a wife and triplets. Can he recover his memory in time to reunite his family for Christmas?

HIS CHRISTMAS REDEMPTION
Three Sisters Ranch • by Danica Favorite

Injured at Christmastime, Erin Drummond must rely on her ex-husband's help caring for her nephews. But as they stay on the ranch together, can Erin and Lance find a way to put their tragic past behind them and reclaim their love?

HOMETOWN CHRISTMAS GIFT
Bent Creek Blessings • by Kat Brookes

The last person widow Lainie Dawson thought to ask for help with her troubled child is her brother's friend Jackson Wade—the man she once loved. But when her son bonds with Jackson and begins to heal, Lainie must confront her past—and future—with the man she never forgot.

LOOK FOR THESE AND OTHER LOVE INSPIRED BOOKS WHEREVER BOOKS ARE SOLD, INCLUDING MOST BOOKSTORES, SUPERMARKETS, DISCOUNT STORES AND DRUGSTORES.

LICNM1019

SPECIAL EXCERPT FROM

HQN™

Surprise fatherhood, Southern charm and a heartwarming family Christmas—read on for a sneak peek at Low Country Christmas, *the conclusion to Lee Tobin McClain's Safe Haven series!*

Cash remembered coming out to Ma Dixie's place at Christmas time growing up. The contrast with his own foster family's home had been extreme. There, six themed Christmas trees were spread throughout the house, decorated perfectly by the commercial operation that brought them out each year and took them away after the holidays. That same company had wrapped garlands around the staircase and strung lights outside the house.

It had all been grand. He remembered being shocked and impressed his first year with the family, because it had been so different from the humble holidays back in Alabama. But he hadn't been allowed to invite his brothers over; too much noise and mess, his foster mother had always said. If he wanted to see them, he had to find a ride out to Ma Dixie's, which he had done frequently.

Here, Christmas really felt like Christmas.

He opened another box of ornaments, pulled out an angel made of hard plastic and handed it to Holly to place on the tree.

"Is this your tree topper, Ma?" Holly asked, holding it up.

"Yes, it is. I usually have Pudge put it up, but...could you do it, Cash, honey?"

He did, easily reaching the top of the small tree. "Is Pudge okay?" he asked Ma. "Is that why the place isn't decorated yet? He's too sick to help?"

Ma arranged the last figures in the Nativity scene and sank down onto the couch. "That's part of it. Mostly, it's me feeling blue. I'm not used to Christmas with no kids around."

Holly tilted her head to one side. "Did you have a lot of kids?"

"Dozens," Ma said with a wide smile. "That's the beauty of being a foster parent."

"Oh," Holly said as she sank down onto an ottoman beside Ma. "Do you…not foster anymore?"

Ma sighed. "I really can't with Pudge having all these doctor appointments. I guess maybe we're getting too old for it." She looked wistfully at the tree. "I just, you know, always enjoyed having the little ones around."

Holly looked thoughtful. "Is that why you wanted to take care of Penny? Not to help me out, but to have a little one around?"

"That's part of it," Ma said, "but don't you worry about it. I understand being picky where your child is concerned."

"It's not pickiness," Holly said. "If I were being picky, who better than an experienced foster parent like you?" She reached out and rubbed Ma's arm back and forth, two or three times, an affectionate gesture that made Ma smile.

Cash came over and sat at Holly's side, leaning against the ottoman. His heart, like that of the Grinch in the movie playing muted on the television, seemed to be expanding.

He'd taken plenty of women to high-end Christmas parties and fancy restaurants. But sitting here in Ma Dixie's house, talking with her about holidays and kids and family problems, decorating the tree with her, felt different. Like coming home.

Like coming home, with Holly beside him.

He put that feeling together with the questions his brother and Pudge had been asking. He was getting the horrifying notion that he might be falling in love with Holly. But he wasn't the falling-in-love type, or the settling-down type. And Holly wasn't the type for a short, superficial fling.

So what exactly was he going to do with all these feelings?

Don't miss Lee Tobin McClain's
Low Country Christmas,
available October 2019 from HQN Books!

Looking for inspiration in tales
of hope, faith and heartfelt romance?

Check out **Love Inspired**® and
Love Inspired® **Suspense** books!

New books available every month!

CONNECT WITH US AT:

Facebook.com/groups/HarlequinConnection

Facebook.com/HarlequinBooks

Twitter.com/HarlequinBooks

Instagram.com/HarlequinBooks

Pinterest.com/HarlequinBooks

ReaderService.com